The Vendetti Family:

Money Murder Mayhem

By: Porschea Jade

1

Acknowledgements

Here we go again. I can't believe I'm at release number two. The feeling is so surreal, but I know that there is nothing else I'd rather be doing than this.

Girls. Everything that mommy does, she does it to make you proud and to better your future. I strive to show you that you can be better than your circumstance because I became so much more than anyone thought I would be. Alani, Elizabeth, Amelia and Paisley, just know that you all give me purpose. I love you to the death of me.

Semaj. Thank you for continuing to ride this rollercoaster with me. I know I'm not the easiest person to get along with and that sometimes you may want to walk away, but I love you for sticking by my side and showing me what it's like to have that love and dedication in me that I sometimes don't feel in myself.

Kellz. You already know that I'm going to continue to ride with you regardless of what anyone else says or feels. You took a chance on me and I can't thank you for that enough. I may annoy you, but just know that we in this thing forevvvvaaaaa. (Cardi B spin) lol. I got mad love for you chick and the sky is the limit.

Rikida. From us being reading partners in a group to us getting close in KKP: Bring Your Own Tea reading group, you have always kept it 1000 with me and I appreciate you from the bottom of my heart. You definitely are a true friend.

To the readers that I gained from *You Give Me Purpose to Love*, I want to thank you from the bottom of my heart for taking a chance on me. Y'all make all of this worthwhile. For the ones that are picking up this one right here, I thank you as well. I hope y'all enjoy this book as much as I enjoyed writing it. I fall in love with all my characters and I hope you will too.

Prologue: Kylani

"The code to the vault isn't working," I said, blowing out a breath of frustration. "Amari, hand me the kit, I'll see if I can crack it open," I told him, attempting to use the code my dad had given us one more time.

I could hear him rummaging through his bag behind me. After a few seconds with no response, I turned around and watched him as he sifted through the contents with a panicked expression on his face.

"What's wrong?"

"Fuck! I forgot it!" he yelled, kicking the bag across the room.

"What do you mean you forgot it? How could you forget the damn kit, Mari?" I questioned as all the air in my lungs seemed to escape in a matter of seconds.

Fuck! I knew something would go wrong, but I didn't think his ass would be dumb enough to forget the case.

"Calm down, La."

"How am I supposed to calm down? You forgot our back-up kit and if we don't come home with whatever is in these safety deposit boxes, then that's our ass! I'm not about to get punished because of your fuck up, Amari."

"Again, calm down La. I got a plan, I packed some C4 just in case I needed it and it looks like we do."

"No. that was not a part of the plan. We're supposed to get in and get out. An explosion will just cause unwanted attention."

"What will be worse? Us blowing open the vault and getting what we came here for, or leaving here empty-handed and having to deal with their wrath? I know I fucked up, but let me make it right," he pleaded with a glimpse of hope in his eyes.

Everything inside of me told me to tell him no and that we should leave, but I knew he would get in far more trouble than me if we went home without completing our mission. So, against my better judgement, I nodded my head and said a quick prayer that everything would be okay.

"Thank you. Now step back."

Crouching underneath the desk behind me, I counted to five and waited for the impact of the blast.

BOOM!

"Come on, I know that triggered the alarm and the police station is only seven minutes away and we have five before time to leave."

Not bothering to respond, I ran in the room searching for the lockbox numbers. As soon as I spotted them, I grabbed the keys my mother gave me and opened all of them one by one as Amari emptied them inside his bag.

Counting to myself, we only had two minutes before we had to be out the door and out the back alley.

"What's that noise?" Amari asked, breaking my concentration.

Listening intently, I silently cursed myself before grabbing the bags off the floor.

"Come on, we have to get out of here now," I told him, running toward the window to look outside.

"Fuck, they blocking the entrance, La. There's no way out of here."

"Yes, there is Now come on. We have forty-five seconds before they come inside," I said over my shoulder as I made my way towards the back staircase of the bank where the employees go to have their meetings.

I'm glad I came in here for weeks prior and just watched their daily hustle and bustle. I used me wanting to get a student loan as my reason for being here so often. When the banker brought me back here earlier this week, I made mental notes of all the emergency exits.

When I reached the doorway to the roof, I went to the edge and looked in the vent to make sure that what I left was still there.

"What you looking for?" Amari questioned nervously.

Bingo!

"Did you ever take those rock climbing lessons like daddy told you to?" I asked, pulling out the grappling hooks and rope.

"No. But why… what the hell are we going to do with that?"

"We're going to climb down. There are only two police cars out front which means maybe four police officers. I know they're looking around on the inside for us because no one is supposed to have a code to the service elevator. So, that gives us about two minutes before they think to look upstairs and we're wasting time. The alley is still empty and Dig is parked two blocks away and these bags are heavy as hell. You have two options at this point. Either you grab this rope and scale down the side of this damn building or you can get caught for robbing a bank. The choice is yours," I told him, staring him square in the eyes.

It took little convincing because he grabbed the extra rope and followed me to the side of the building.

"Here, take these," I said, handing him the extra gloves I had in my hand.

Taking a deep breath, I prayed we didn't break a bone as I holstered the bags on my back and climbed down the side of the building with Amari right behind me.

"Man, La we're three fucking stories up. What happens if we fall?" Amari questioned, looking down at me.

"Shut up and man up. If we fall we'll break something, but we'll be fine. Now hurry," I told him, rolling my eyes.

I swear, Amari walked around as if he was the toughest thing made since Teflon, but he was scared of heights. Groaning internally, I focused on getting down this building so we could get as far away from here as possible.

As soon as our feet hit the ground, we took off running towards where the car was supposed to be waiting. When the car came into view, I breathed a sigh of relief that we made it out. The thought of college was sounding better and better by the minute. I can't keep living my life like this.

Chapter 1: Kylani

One month later...

"Happy birthday, baby cakes!" my dad smiled as he came in to my room. I had just put on my PINK! Joggers and sports bra so I could take my morning run.

"Good morning, daddy. Thank you," I smiled, pulling my hair into a bun before turning around to look at the breakfast tray he had in his hand.

"Awww daddy, you didn't have to fix me breakfast. I was going to grab a muffin and some orange juice before my run."

"You will not. Here, I made your favorites, a bowl of mixed fruits, egg whites, two pieces of turkey bacon, fresh squeezed orange juice and I even put a blueberry muffin on there for you," he told me, winking at me before sitting it on the end of my bed.

Looking up at my dad, all I could do was smile. I know a lot of girls say they are daddy's girls, but I truly was. My dad was my first true love other than Amari. As he would say, I was his princess. People often told me I was a darker version of my mother, but I was my father's child through and through. My dad stood about 6'5 with a bald head and a full beard. He was the color of dark toffee and built like a linebacker. I may have had my mother's features, but I got my strong will and personality from him.

"Thank you again, daddy." I kissed him on the cheek before sitting down on my bed to eat.

"Whenever you finish eating, stop by my office before you go on your run. I want to talk to you about something."

"Okay."

It took about ten minutes to eat all my food. I took my dirty dishes in the kitchen and rinsed them off before putting them in the dishwasher and headed to the study. I never really came in here unless we had family meetings or dad was giving us new assignments. The first time I was in here, I had just turned sixteen and my dad wanted me to go along with my mom on a jewelry heist. I was nervous at first, but after a while I got used to it.

As I made it to the door, I heard muffled voices from the other side. I knew it had to be my mother. Mentally preparing myself, I knocked on the door and waited patiently for someone to open it.

"It's open, come in."

Walking in to the room, I saw that my mom and dad weren't alone. Amari and his friend Rylan were also there. Rylan was the same age as my brother. They were both nineteen. On the outside, his appearance seemed as if he wouldn't harm a fly, but he creeped me out. He would just watch me while we trained and whenever I walked around the house. I had told my dad about it once before, but he told me I was probably just being paranoid and that he was just quiet by nature. I listened to what my dad told me, but it didn't stop me from keeping an eye on him. You could say he was the other son my parents never had. He was the son of my dad's old business partner, Ramon. When he took a fifteen-year bid for my dad a few years ago, my parents promised they would look after him and that's what they've been doing ever since.

As soon as everyone in the room noticed my presence, they stopped talking abruptly and all the hairs on the back of my neck stood up.

"How was your breakfast?" my dad asked, turning away from whatever conversation he was having with my mom.

Bouncing my eyes between the two, I could see that whatever they were talking about my mom didn't like it by the way her face was balled up.

"It was great. Thank you again."

"So, you walk into the room and all you see is him?"

Groaning inwardly, I counted to ten in my head before I turned towards her.

"Good morning, mama. Amari, Rylan."

I don't know why she was always a bitch to me because she treated Amari better than people treated the Pope. It bothered me in the beginning because what girl doesn't want her mother's love, but after a while I ignored it and focused on being me. I would never be a mama's girl, and that was fine too.

"Leave her alone, Leilani. Now, everyone have a seat so I can get this over with," my dad instructed, pointing towards the empty chairs around the room.

Doing as told, I took a seat on the chair next to me and waited for whatever he had to say.

"As you all know, I've spent years grooming someone to take over the family business. I'm getting older and I want to enjoy the fruits of my labor, but I can't do that planning bank robberies and jewelry heists. With Amari being the oldest and only male, it would only be right that I hand over the family business to him. However, I feel it would be best if Kylani was trained to be the next head of this family."

"WHAT?!" we all said in unison.

The look of anger and shock on Amari's face couldn't be missed, and my mom was looking at him as if he lost his mind.

Me? The next head of the family?

"Dad, what do you mean you want La to be the next head of the family? I'm older than her! She should take over after I step down. I've been working my ass off doing all these jobs with Rylan so that when do I take over, he would be my second in command. This is bullshit!" Amari yelled, jumping up.

"Sit down Amari before I knock you down. You will respect me in my house, and if it wasn't for her your dumb ass would be in jail right now! Or have you already forgotten the night of bank robbery a month ago?" he asked as his eyes shot daggers at Amari, silently daring him to say something else. Taking the hint, Amari folded his arms and said nothing else.

"Now, as I was saying, I want Kylani to take over my spot as the head of the Vendetti Crime Family, but I'm not just handing it over to her. She has to prove that she is fit to run this organization as I have for years, if not better."

"Kye, think about what you're saying. She's just a little girl, she's not ready for this. I think it's best that we give the family business over to Amari as planned," my mom, said trying to convince him he was making a bad decision.

"Yea, dad. Maybe they're right… I'm only eighteen, as of today I might add. How am I supposed to take over? I mean, maybe…"

"Enough, La," he said, holding his hand up, cutting me off.

"My decision is final. Kylani, you will start your training to take over just as your brother has. And Amari, you will have to prove that you are the better person to lead this family. Now, do you both understand me?" he questioned, looking back and forth at us.

"Yes, sir."

"Good. Now everyone else can leave. I need to speak to La alone please."

When everyone was gone, we just sat and stared at each other for a few minutes before he finally broke the silence.

"Why didn't you tell me you applied for an out of state college?"

Out of all the things he could have said, I didn't expect for him to say that. Trying to find my words, I kept opening and closing my mouth in an attempt to formulate a sentence. When no words came out, I lowered my head because I knew I was caught.

"Lift your head up, Kylani. I'm disappointed because you didn't tell me, but you should never bow your head to anyone. Not even me."

"Honestly, I didn't know how to tell you. I know how you feel about the family business and I wasn't sure that bringing up that I wanted to leave California and go down South for college was the best thing to do until after I graduated this summer."

"I need you to train to take over the family business."

"But why? Amari is next in line to take over once you step down. Why would you want me to?" I questioned, genuinely confused.

"It's simple. I know you're better suited to take over for me. I'm not just saying it because you're my favorite either," he told me, cracking a smile. I giggled with him a little until he cleared his throat and straightened up, getting serious again.

"Truthfully, Kylani, I knew that you were the perfect person to take over for me when you were thirteen-years-old."

"How?"

"You remember when you spent the entire day with me and Ramon riding around the city? We were in and out the office all day?" he asked.

"Yes, because we were supposed to go out to a movie and to get ice cream, but we never got a chance to because you had to run off and do something with Mr. Ramon."

"Do you remember what happened?" he asked, staring at me.

"Of course. When we got there he was going on and on about losing the bank account numbers and codes for a job that you two had later on that night."

"And what did you do?"

"I wrote down all the numbers for him on a piece of paper."

"But how?" he pressed.

"I saw the paper earlier that week in a file you left open on the kitchen counter. At first I wouldn't give him the paper because I thought I would get in trouble, but when I finally did, you both were so happy."

"Exactly. I knew then you were smarter than any of us combined. Don't get me wrong, your brother is borderline genius and has what it takes to be great, but he's impulsive. He acts before he thinks when his anger is involved and that will be his downfall. You and your brother are complete opposites. Everything he lacks you have and then some, but you've always wanted more," he explained. "I'll make a deal with you," he started.

"Okay?" I answered with hesitation.

"Spend the rest of your school year and this summer truly training to take over the family business. I want you to put your heart, blood, sweat and tears into taking over, and if in the end Amari is better suited for the job, then I will let you go to an out of state college. But, if I see that you are the better candidate, then I need you to step up to the plate and run this family."

"But…"

"Listen, Kylani. I know it's asking a lot from you especially with you being so young, but I need you to do this for me. Sometimes, you have to believe in someone that doesn't quite believe in themselves yet. I know you can make this empire great again. It may not make sense now why this is so important to me, but one day it will."

Thinking over his proposal, I weighed the pros and cons of what he was asking me to do. On one hand, I knew that this wasn't what I wanted, but on the other, I knew how much this meant to him. I didn't see myself becoming the next head of the family when I knew Amari could step up and take over, but I would honor my dad's request. What's the worst that could happen, right?

After I agreed, we talked for thirty more minutes about the next assignment that Amari and I were set to go on, which was the same day as my graduation. I prayed my decision didn't come back to bite me in the ass later on down the road.

Chapter 2: Blue

At the tender age of twenty-three, I had seen more in this world than people twice my age. My mom was a crack whore by the name of Linda and my dad ran the Trinidad cartel and moved anything from cocaine to human body parts on the Black Market. The name Blanco rang bells everywhere in the States, and even overseas. Raised out in Georgia with my Aunt Mia, I was thirteen when my dad came around and taught me to follow his path. The world hardened my heart a long-time ago, and if it wasn't about money I wasn't trying to hear it. I was as ruthless as they came and would murder you and your whole family all while sleeping like a baby at night. Call me what you want, but Blue is what the streets call me.

My government name is Orion Alvarez, but I got the name Blue because of the large amounts of ecstasy I moved along the Southern parts of Georgia and Alabama along with the midnight blue 2014 Malibu that I drove. I dibbled and dabbed in a bit of everything, but I saw a majority of my money through pill pushing. Pills weren't just a street drug and that's what I loved about it. I could sell it to a pill head on the streets or to the rich kids in Buckhead. Either way, I saw a profit. I was getting it by any means necessary, but I would never forget where I came from. I didn't see myself slowing down anytime soon. I just wanted to stack my chips, and when I was content then I would build my aunt the house of her dreams and settle down and find a chick to start a family with.

"Dammit, Blue, why didn't you tell me you were about to nut? You got that shit all on my face and in my hair. If it's messed up, you're paying to get it fixed," Shauna whined.

I swear, all shorty did was complain. She could talk all that shit if she wanted to, but I wasn't paying for shit. Hoe should have kept my dick in her mouth and she wouldn't have to worry about my nut in her hair.

"Yea, whatever shorty. Go get me a warm rag. I got somewhere I need to be in half an hour," I told her, grabbing my Note 4 off the night stand to see if I had any missed calls or texts.

Sucking her teeth, she rolled out the bed and headed to the bathroom. I hated her attitude, but she was bad as hell. Standing about 5'4, she had smooth dark brown skin and a big enough ass to feed a third world country. Shorty was ghetto as they came, she put me in the mind of that stripper Cardi B, but it was something about a ghetto broad that turned me on. When all that slick shit they were popping got on my nerves, I'd stick all these inches down the back of their throats. I'd never wife one, but they knew how to suck a mean dick and take all of it in without all that whining and complaining. I ain't got the biggest dick in the world, but my shit is big enough to fuck with. Eight and a half inches of pure caramel.

I stood 6'4 and weighed 235 pounds. I wasn't skinny, but I wasn't fat either. I had a medium build and tattoos littered my neck, chest and back that I loved to show off. Even though I knew females fucked with me because I wasn't an ugly nigga, it was my smile and dimples that caught their attention every time.

Shauna wiping me down made my dick throb, and I had to remind myself that I had a flight to catch within the next few hours. If that wasn't the case, I would have let her rock my mic one time for the road.

"When will you be back over to see me?" she asked, popping her gum in my ear.

"You'll know whenever I pop up. I'm up," I told her, pulling my pants up.

"Well, call before you come. I may find me a new nigga before you decide to come back around. I won't wait around for you, Blue."

She said that shit like it was supposed to make me hot or something, but she played herself because I couldn't care less. She wasn't my bitch. It is what it is.

"Do you, ma," I said laughing as I made my way out the door.

Stepping out of her apartment, I spotted my right hand man Zane chopping it up with some little chicken head from around the way. When he saw me headed in their direction, he igged her ass and met me half way.

"Almighty Blue, what's good my nigga?" he joked, dabbing me up.

"I can't call it. You ready to head out to Cali?" I asked, leaning against the hood of my car.

"You already know it. I'm trying to bag me one of them West Coast bitches so when I get tired of this country ass shit, I got somewhere to go."

"Yeen' lying. I got a bitch in every area I frequent except Cali. I wouldn't mind finding one to kick it with when I'm that way," I told him, stroking my goatee.

We sat around joking until it was time to catch our flight. My dad had some shit out that way he wanted me to check out, and as always I was on the first thing smoking. Blanco had a lot of enemies so there was no telling who tried to get at him, but I planned to find out before I left.

* * * *

The seven-hour flight had me ready to lay down, but that wasn't an option. I was ready to get this meeting over with so I could fuck something, eat and go to sleep. In that order. Jumping into the car that was waiting on me and Zane, I prepared myself for the forty-five-minute drive out to my dad's compound.

I hated that he always had a driver waiting for me like I wasn't a grown ass man, but this was his way of making sure we weren't followed so I tolerated it. Arriving to his spot, I took in my surroundings. As usual, he had bitches walking around half naked and there were a few people I recognized here and there. I wasn't the social type so I hit them with a head nod and kept it moving.

"There's my boy!"

Turning toward his voice, I scanned my surroundings until my eyes landed on him, and I headed over in his direction.

"What's up old man?" I joked, pulling him into a half hug.

"You wish you look this good when you get my age," he laughed before turning his attention to Zane.

"Zane, how are you?"

"You know me. Same old, same old."

"Follow me. We have some business to discuss."

You wouldn't know that my dad was from the islands unless he was mad or he told you. All his years in the States had helped his broken English. His accent was still there, but you could understand what he was saying. Walking through the house, I saw twice as many bitches in here than were outside. I knew my dad was fucking at least one if not all of them. I don't know what it was, but females loved my dad. From what my aunt told me, island men were straight up whores and my dad proved that to be true time and time again. She told me that his singsong voice got my mom at hello and that's why she was so far gone over him all those years they were together.

"Have a seat," he instructed, taking a seat behind his cherry oak desk.

Doing as I was told, I stifled a yawn and waited for him to say what he had to say.

"I saw Linda."

Snapping my head up, I just stared at him for a few minutes. He knew I hated when he brought her up, but he did it every time I came around.

"What you telling me for?" I seethed.

"Because dats your mother. She asked about you."

"She ain't got no reason to be worried about me now. I'm grown, it's a little late to be concerned about my well-being. She couldn't care less about me when she left me on Auntie Mia's front porch for hours in the snow with only a thin t-shirt and jeans on when I was seven while she chased her next high."

"Dammit, Orion! You're gonna have to forgive her someday."

"Na, I'll pass. Now, I know you didn't call me all this way to talk about her, so what's up?" I asked, changing the subject.

Shaking his head at me, he grabbed two folders and handed them to both me and Zane.

"What's this?" Zane asked as he flipped through the pictures.

"That is Leilani and Amari Vendetti. They are a part of an underground organization called the Vendetti Crime Family," he explained.

"Okay, but what does this have to do with you?" I questioned, confused.

I didn't see how this boy and lady were significant to my day and his business.

"Flip to the next page."

The next picture was of a tall, dark skin man with a bald head and full beard. Now I was really confused because as many times as I had come to Cali I had never seen him, but then again I wasn't looking for him either.

"Who is he?"

"That's Kye."

"You mean Cocaine Kye, the one that married that mafia princess?" Zane questioned.

"Yep, the same one."

"No wonder the name sounded so familiar."

"Okay, I'm still confused. Can someone please explain who the hell these people are and what they got to do with why we here?" I snapped. They're over here talking in riddles and I just wanted to go to sleep.

"The Vendetti family runs the majority of everything illegal that comes this way other than myself. Kye was once my best friend when I first came to the States, but the falling out with his dad made him my enemy."

When he saw he had our undivided attention, he continued.

"Kye's father, Meiko, was training Kye to take over his drug business when he met Leilani. Meiko knew the Feds were closing in on him and that he was going away for a long time, but the more time Kye spent with Leilani, the less focused he was with taking over his father's drug business. My father and his father were friends and business partners. My dad supplied the cocaine and his dad brought it into the States. When Meiko saw that Kye wasn't focused, he taught me the ropes instead. A few weeks into my training, his father's house got raided and the police took him into custody. I tried calling Kye for hours to tell him what happened, but he didn't show his face until days later."

"So basically you took over the business that was rightfully his?" I questioned.

"Yes. While his dad was getting arraigned, he was off two cities away eloping with Leilani. His father disowned him and handed everything over to me. With my dad being the supplier, taking over and expanding his empire was a piece of cake, and within a few years I had expanded out past the West Coast and was working my way out East. I offered him a partnership because I understood it was rightfully his, but he cursed me and started a war between the Italians and the Trinidad cartel because his feelings were hurt. That was twenty-six years ago and he's still trying every way he can to bring down the empire that his father built. About a month ago, he sent his son and daughter into the bank to steal 6.2 million dollars' worth of diamonds that I had deposited weeks prior."

"His daughter?" I asked, looking back down at the folder in my hands.

Turning to the next set of pictures, I saw one of the prettiest females I had seen in a minute. From the pictures I could tell she was young, but the way she carried herself was something unheard of.

She had to be about 5'7 with smooth, milk chocolate skin. She had slanted eyes and long curly black hair that flowed down her back. She had a medium build with nice toned thighs and a nice sized chest. Maybe a C cup. She looked kind of tomboyish because in every picture she was showing off her six-pack in some kind of way, but it fit her.

Glancing over at Zane, he had the same confused expression that I did.

"You want me to believe that this girl is into robbing banks and jewelry heists?" I questioned, looking back down at the pictures.

"That "girl" as you call her, is responsible for pulling off one of the biggest heists of her parents' career just a short time ago. Don't judge a book by its cover," he advised.

After he finished his story, I sat quietly flipping through the pictures and studied everything in the folder.

"So, what do you want us to do?" Zane was the first to speak up.

"Here's what I need you to do…"

I still felt that there had to be more to the story than just old friends rivaling over territory. Twenty-six years is a long time to hold a grudge, but I knew how delicate a man's ego was and for his father to basically spit in his face and hand his best friend over everything that was his would crush any man. For now, I would follow my dad's lead, but I wasn't trying to become a part of something that was never mine to begin with.

Chapter 3: Kylani

The weeks were winding down until semester break and I was trying to ace my mid-terms so I could prepare for my summer classes at Modesto Junior. I did agree to train this summer, but I wouldn't stop my studies. That was out of the question. I could just transfer my credits when the time came. Stopping to catch my breath, I checked my watch to see how fast I ran my first mile.

Damn, eight minutes and twenty-seven seconds.

My best time was seven minutes, twenty-two seconds, so I was definitely slipping. Taking a drink of my water, I prepared myself to take off on my second mile when I felt something slam into my back, knocking me off my feet and sending me flying to the ground.

"Ahh, my fault. Let me help you up," the voice said from over me.

"Don't! I got it. You should watch where you're going," I growled as I checked to see how bad I was bleeding before standing up to dust myself off. There were a few scrapes, but nothing major.

"I said I was sorry. I was looking down at my watch and I didn't see you."

"You said it was your fault, not that you were sorry, but no hard feelings. You're making me run behind and I have somewhere to be after this so I have to go."

"Damn, are you always this cold?"

"Excuse me?" I asked, looking up for the first time, and I swear when I did the world stood still for a second. Corny I know, but he was just that fine. He had to be at least 8 inches taller than me with smooth, caramel skin and a head full of deep waves. When he noticed me staring at him, he smirked and I almost lost it. He had the prettiest set of teeth I had seen on anyone with deep dimples to match. My heart rate detector bracelet on my wrist started beeping and my cheeks got hot.

"Did you hear me, ma?"

"Ummm. No. I'm sorry, what did you say?" I asked, breaking eye contact with him.

"I noticed your knee was bleeding and I asked if you could move it?"

"It's fine. Look, I have to go," I told him, jogging in the opposite direction.

"Wait up!" he yelled, catching up to me.

"What could you possibly want?" I questioned, stealing glances at him out the corner of my eye as we ran.

"What's your name?"

"Why?"

"Damn. I guess you are always this cold," he chuckled, keeping up with my pace.

I could tell by the quick once over of his body that he was fit and could probably run laps around me, but for some reason he slowed it down to my pace.

"I'm sorry. I'm just not used to strange men knocking me down, inviting themselves to run with me and then asking me questions, so excuse me if I come off as rude." I rolled my eyes sarcastically.

"My name is Orion, but you can call me Blue," he introduced himself, completely ignoring my snide remark.

Ignoring him, I kept running my mile thinking to myself how fine he was the whole time. I was never the type to drool over boys. I was always so focused on school and my extra-curricular activities that I didn't have time to entertain anyone, but there was something different about this one. I could tell he was older than me even if only by a few years, but his air of confidence spoke volumes and made him seem older. We ran the remainder of the mile in silence. As soon as we rounded the last corner, I saw the last person I expected to see at the park. Rylan. It was odd because he never came to the natural trail.

"Kylani!"

I was tempted to ignore him as if I didn't see him standing there, but when he started jogging in our direction I knew that was out of question.

"What's up, Ry? What are you doing here?"

"I came looking for you. Who's your friend?" he questioned, staring Orion up and down.

"Blue," he said, holding his hand out to shake Rylan's.

After a few seconds of awkward silence, Rylan finally shook his hand. There was something in Rylan's eyes that I had never seen before. He felt threatened by Blue. I could tell by the way he kept diverting his eyes from his and wouldn't meet his gaze for too long. My dad always said watch out for the ones that don't meet your gaze, they always had something to hide. Shaking his head slightly, Orion chuckled before turning in my direction.

"It was nice meeting you. I gotta get going, but I hope to see you around again soon," he said, smiling down at me before kissing me on my forehead and walking away.

I watched him confused as ever because he didn't know me from a can of paint, but he felt comfortable enough to kiss me on my forehead. I didn't speak more than ten sentences to him the whole time we were in each other's presence.

"Who was that guy, La?" Rylan asked, snapping me out of my thoughts.

"Just some guy I met today. I fell and my knee was feeling a little funny so he offered to run with me to make sure I was okay."

I wasn't sure why I lied, but something told me that Rylan would make more of the situation if I told him the truth and I didn't need him running back telling Amari and my dad anything. Grabbing my bags off the bench, I prepared myself to get dressed and go to the library to study for my last exam that I had later on this week. My mind drifted back to Orion and I had this feeling I would see him again very soon.

Chapter 4: Amari

My dad telling me that he felt that Kylani should take over the family business instead of me was like a punch in the gut. Being the oldest and only son, the business was to be turned over to me when he stepped down, but now I had to compete with La for something that was rightfully mine to begin with. I had to convince her to tell dad that she didn't want it and to give everything over to me.

I knew how much she wanted to go off to college and live life as a normal teenager and I would use that to my advantage at a later time, but for now we were preparing for one of our biggest heists yet. As much as I didn't want to admit it, I needed Kylani's help. La's intellect was something out of this world. Don't get it twisted though, I was the valedictorian of my graduating class, but La was special. I've watched her study a paper once and remember everything on it without second guessing herself and in this line of work, she was a major asset to the team. I just don't feel she's fit to run it. I had been preparing to take over since I was eight and I wouldn't stand by and watch it be snatched from underneath me by my baby sister.

I was so caught up in my thoughts, I didn't hear Rylan when he came into the indoor basketball court that was in the basement of our house.

"What you up to?"

"Just shooting hoops to clear my head. What's up with you?" I asked, walking over to the chair and taking a sip of my water.

"Do you know if La has a boyfriend?"

That shit came from complete left field. I always knew Rylan had a thing for La, but she never paid him any attention. To be honest, she avoided him as much as she could and only interacted with him when she was forced to.

"You know La ain't that type. I've never even seen her look at guys. She's more focused on her books so she can get into a good college. Why you ask?"

"I ran into her at the park earlier this week…"

"Since when do you go to the park?" I interrupted.

"I was meeting that chick Kaye up there and I ended up seeing La, but that's beside the point. Anyway, I saw La running with some tall ass light skinned dude."

"Did you ask her about it?"

"Yeah. I walked over to them and asked her who he was and he introduced himself as Blue or some shit like that. When he left I asked her who he was and she told me that she fell and he offered to run with her because her knee was messed up," he explained.

I racked my mind trying to see if I knew anyone by the name of Blue, but I came up empty. Rylan was most likely jealous that he'd seen someone else in La's face that wasn't him.

"Well, maybe that's what happened. Again, you know La's not into dating and she hates liars, so why would she lie to you about something so small as a guy in the park?" I asked, scrolling through my text messages on my phone.

"Amari, you not hearing me, though. You didn't see him. Dude had tattoos all over his body and was built like that one football player, Odell Beckman Jr. I could tell she was feeling him from the way she was staring at him."

"I think you're just jealous, man. Look, I got to go. My dad wants to go over these plans for this truck job," I told him as I got up.

"Alright. I needed to be heading to work anyway. I didn't get this job driving these armored trucks for Loomis to get fired before we even get a chance to do the job," he said, dabbing me up.

"Alright, man. I'm up."

I made a mental note to ask La another time about the mystery man from the park, but I'm sure Ry was making it out to be more than what it was. I had more important shit to worry about, so who ever she was or wasn't dating wasn't on my list of priorities. On second thought, maybe La having a little boyfriend is exactly what she needs to distract her from taking over. Either way it went, I was prepared to do whatever I needed to ensure that I won because if not, I was willing to destroy it. If I wasn't the next head of the family, then no one would be. It was just that simple.

Chapter 5: Blue

The pictures I saw did baby girl no justice at all. She was a fine little thing. I was tempted to get her number the other day, but I had to tell myself that this was just business. Besides, the way her attitude was set up, I doubt if she would have given it to me anyway. I've always been a good judge of character and even though she was a little rude, I could tell she had a good heart which confused me because she was nothing like the ruthless young girl my dad painted her out to be.

Pushing the thoughts to the back of my head, I prepared to leave my apartment and head over to scoop up Zane from his new spot so we could go furniture shopping. I know what you're thinking, what thug goes shopping for furniture, but that's where you're wrong. For one, I'm not a thug, just a young nigga trying to make a living. And two, I have a sense of style about myself and I couldn't have my house looking any kind of way.

Pulling up at Zane's spot, I beeped the horn twice and waited for him to come down. Zane stayed over by some collegiate school or something. He said he needed to be close to some potential female victims and all I could do was laugh because I knew he was serious. Glancing in the direction of his apartments, someone caught my eye and I knew God was on my side. It was shorty from the park. Jumping out of my car, I jogged across the street in the direction she was coming from.

"Ayo, La!" I yelled to get her attention.

Stopping in her tracks, she looked back in my direction and all I could do was smile and bite my lip. Shorty had the whole Aaliyah tomboy look down. She had on baggy, olive colored cargo pants with her briefs showing, a cut-off baby doll shirt that displayed her six pack and wheat colored Timberlands. To pull it all together, she had her hair in some kind of messy looking bun. I swear, baby girl is the truth.

"Hey, what's up?" I smiled down at her when I was within arm's length.

"Hey."

She was so soft-spoken, but I thought it was cute. I glanced back in the direction of my car to see if Zane had come out the house, but when I saw he hadn't, I turned my attention back to her and caught her giving me the once over. A young nigga was fresh in my white jeans, black Polo collar shirt, black and white plaid Polo kicks and a black Polo fitted cap. I didn't wear them often, but I even had my bottom gold slugs in my mouth giving off the hood persona.

"Are you following me?"

Laughing a little, I shook my head before answering her.

"Nah, this is a complete coincidence. I was actually over this way picking up my homeboy so we could do a little shopping. Seeing you was just a plus."

"Mm hmm. How would you call that a plus and you don't even know me?" she questioned, raising her eyebrow.

"Because I get to see your pretty face. Now, if you let me get your number then that would make my whole day."

"I don't know you well enough to give you my number. You could be a stalker or something, and right now you look real suspect."

"I ain't gotta stalk you, ma. Give it a few months and you won't be able to get enough of the kid," I smirked at her.

"Oh, really?"

"Yea, really. I'm liable to fuck up your whole life."

"If you say so, but hey I have to go. I actually have to get to my next class. I have mid-terms this week and if I don't pass this exam, it'll mess up my GPA going into the next semester," she said, glancing down at her watch.

"Beauty and brains, I like it. Well, I'll let you go on one condition," I told her, reaching out and grabbing her hand before she could walk away.

"And what's that?" she asked, staring at my hand as if it was contaminated or something.

"Meet me at the park tomorrow for a run."

After thinking it over for a moment, she nodded her head.

"Be there at 5 in the morning sharp," she responded, taking her hand out of mine.

"I'll be there."

"Don't be late, Orion," she said over her shoulder as she walked away.

"Oh, you remember my name, huh?"

Turning around to walk backwards, she gave me this half smirk that made my dick hard.

"Yea something like that, but bye, I have to go. See you in the morning." She broke into a full smile before pivoting and running away.

I stared off in the direction that she went in before heading back towards my car.

"What was all that about?" Zane asked as soon as I made it back across the street. I was so caught up replaying our little conversation that I didn't even notice Zane leaning against the hood staring at us.

"That my friend, was Kylani," I told him, getting in the driver's seat.

"The girl from the pictures?"

"Yea, that's her," I said, starting up my car.

"I hope you know what you're doing, Blue," Zane warned, shaking his head.

I brushed off his comment. Zane is my boy and I know he worries about me, but I had the situation with La under control. Changing the direction of our conversation, we went over our plans about setting up shop down here but the whole time we were talking my mind kept drifting back to the smile that La gave me before she ran off. I was more excited about tomorrow morning than I should be. I had to keep reminding myself that this was just about business, but in the back of my head I knew it could turn into more than that if I wasn't careful. As crazy as it sounds, La had the potential to make a nigga change his ways and I barely even knew her. She was just different and that was like a breath of fresh air. I was fascinated by baby girl, but I would never admit that out loud to anyone, not even myself. I just hope I can stay focused and pull this mission off with no problems.

Chapter 6: Kylani

Seeing Orion right before class had my mind in a million and two different places. He looked better today than he did that day in the park day and his voice alone made my center thump uncontrollably.

"Ms. Vendetti, could you please repeat for me the last part of my lesson since you are obviously too preoccupied drawing in your notebook to pay attention?" Professor Sanders said, snatching me out of my daydream.

I maintained the highest GPA in our senior class other than this Asian girl named Kathrine, but for some strange reason he always gave me a hard time. It was as if he had a personal vendetta against me. I felt that my level of intelligence bothered him because I didn't have to work as hard as everyone else. It wasn't my fault though, it just came naturally.

"Ms. Vendetti, I'm waiting."

"You were going over…"

"No. At the front of the classroom, please."

Rolling my eyes, I got up and walked to the front of the class where the blackboard was.

"You were going over how to solve the equation on the board," I told him, shifting from one foot to the other.

"Okay, well you obviously already know how to solve the equation, so why don't you teach the rest of the class? Since you don't need to know the material on the exam."

I knew he was testing me more than anything, but instead of responding I picked up the chalk and soled the problem. When I put the chalk back down I faced him.

"The answer is 7."

"How… How did you…?" he stammered. He looked genuinely surprised as he double checked my answer in the answer book.

"As you said before, I already knew the answer," I responded just as the bell rang.

Walking back over to my desk, I felt everyone's eyes on me but I ignored them as I grabbed my backpack and headed towards the door.

"She's creepy as hell, I swear. She's always just watching people. I don't see how she's related to Amari's fine ass," I heard this girl named Brittani say from behind me, but I was used to it by now.

I was quiet by nature and I didn't mingle with crowds. That was more of my brother's thing than mine. He loved being the life of the party, but I just didn't like people in general. Girls were too catty for me and guys only wanted me because they thought of me as some kind of conquest because I was still a virgin. I just wanted to focus on finishing as the Salutatorian of the graduating class of 2015. Everything else was irrelevant.

* * * *

For the rest of the day, I focused on studying and training for this heist we had coming up a few months after my graduation. As much as I tried to keep my life on track, I always felt my life was hanging in the balance and the unknown bothered me the most.

"What you doing down here?"

Closing my eyes for a moment, I allowed my body to drop to the ground from the bar I was doing my pull-ups on. My mom never came into the playroom unless she was with my dad, but for her to be here alone only meant she was looking for me specifically.

"I was training like I do every night," I responded, grabbing the towel off the chair beside me and wiping the sweat that was dripping down my face.

"Don't get smart with me, Kylani!"

"No one is getting smart with you. You asked me a question, and I gave you an answer."

"Don't make me slap the taste out of your mouth. I am your mother and you will respect me."

"Yea, barely," I mumbled under my breath. I must've said it louder than I expected because as soon as the words left my mouth, I felt her walking in my direction.

"What the hell did you just say?"

"Nothing," I said, looking at her.

"No, you so grown. Say it again, so I can smack you down where you stand."

As much as she disrespected me and we bumped heads, I would never blatantly disrespect her, but at this moment she was testing my patience.

"I didn't say anything."

"That's what I thought, but I came down here because I need to talk to you."

"About?" I asked skeptically.

"You telling your father that you want him to hand over the business to Amari."

"And why would you want me to do that?"

"Because you can't run this business alone. Just look at you. You're just a little girl wanting to play cops and robbers," she said like it was supposed to be obvious.

"Besides, the business is rightfully his to begin with. You aren't built to run a multimillion dollar empire. You think you're too good for this life anyway. Oh, don't look so surprised, your brother told me all about how you were venting to him saying you wanted to be a normal teenager and go off to college. Well, now's your chance. Tell your father you don't want to run the business and I'll personally pay for you to go to an out of state college."

Staring at her, I tried to figure out what I could have possibly done for her to be such a bitch to me my whole life, and I realized she was just bitter as hell for no reason.

"I can't do that," I said, attempting to walk past her. As far as I was concerned, this conversation was over.

"Oh you can, and you will."

"And if I don't?" I challenged with my back still facing her.

"I'll make you regret it," she whispered in my ear before walking past me headed towards the door.

I wasn't sure at the time what her threat meant, but at this point it made me want to show her that I was more than she thought I was. I was the strongest and smartest person on the team and I was more than ready to prove it.

Chapter 7: Blue

The next morning, I beat my alarm clock up and I was trying to figure out why I was so pressed to see lil mama again. There was something about her presence that did something to me. I couldn't explain it. Hopping in the shower, I took a quick ten-minute shower before throwing on my running gear which consisted of some sweat pants, a black beater and my Puma running shoes.

After fixing a breakfast smoothie, I was out the door and headed to the park to meet up with La. I pulled up at 4:50 and she was already there stretching. I watched her for a few minutes before getting out to join her.

"Good morning," I greeted her.

"Morning," she smiled and continued stretching.

"So, how far are we running?"

"Ummm… I usually run two miles, but if that's too much we can do one."

"What you trying to say, ma? That I can't run two miles with you?" I asked, raising my eyebrow as I looked down at her.

"I didn't say that, but we'll see," she said smirking.

"Okay. How about we make a little wager then?"

"What did you have in mind?"

"If I win, you have to give me your number and take me out to breakfast."

"Okay. That's fair enough, and if I win you have to quit following me. Deal?" she asked, extending out her hand to shake mine.

"I told you before I'm not following you, but whatever you say," I said shaking her hand.

"Okay. On your mark. Get set. Go!" she yelled before taking off in a full run.

Running around this park with her was tiring as hell, but I kept up with her. During the last quarter mile, I showed off and sprinted the whole way back to our starting point.

"I won," I told her when she made it over to me a few seconds later.

"Yea, because you cheated."

"Never that, ma. Now, a deal's a deal."

"Fine. What do you want for breakfast?" she asked, taking a sip of her water.

"I'm thinking IHOP, but we can go somewhere else if you want," I replied, pulling my shirt over my head.

"Uh… yea, IHOP is fine."

Looking in her direction, I tried to figure out what had her stumbling over her words when I caught her staring at my eight-pack.

"See something you like?"

"Huh?"

"You were staring, so I asked if you see something you like."

"No one was staring at you," she said turning her head.

"You ain't gotta lie, but okay, I'll let you make it for now," I said winking at her.

"Whatever. Come on."

"Where you going?"

"Over to my jeep," she said, pointing towards a powder-purple 2015 Jeep Cherokee.

I don't know who she thought she was about to drive around in that, but it damn sure wouldn't be me. What I look like riding around in a light purple car?

"I'm not getting in that."

"Well, I guess you can walk," she sassed with a shrug of her shoulders and walked towards her jeep.

"Na, lil mama. You riding with me," I said, making my way in her direction.

"I'm not getting in the car with you. I barely know you."

"Wrong answer," I said, scooping her up and throwing her over my shoulder.

"Put me down! Are you crazy?" she yelled, kicking and screaming.

The few people that were there looked at us crazy, but I didn't care. Fuck them.

"I'll put you down when we get to my car."

"If you don't put me down in the next five seconds, you will regret it."

"And what you gonna do if I don't?"

Next thing I knew, a sharp pain shot through my back and I almost threw her ass clean across the parking lot. This bitch bit me. Taking her from off my shoulder, I sat her down on the hood of my car. She better be glad I made it to my car or I would have dropped her on the ground instead.

Stepping between her legs, I wrapped them around my waist before picking her back up and pressed her body against my driver's door.

"What are you doing?"

"Did you just bite me?" I asked, ignoring her question.

"I told you to put me down," she retorted, sucking her teeth.

"Okay," I told her before biting the hell out her shoulder.

"Owwww! Why would you do that?" she cried out.

"Because you bit me first. Hell, I bite back. Don't bite me, I won't bite you," I told her shrugging my shoulders.

"What if I slapped you, will you slap me back?" she asked, looking me dead in my eyes.

"It's a possibility, but if I slapped you trust me you'd like it," I smirked, bringing my face close to hers.

I almost forgot that I had her legs wrapped around my waist, but when I said that, I felt her center thumping against my abs and the heat radiating off of it. Wanting to see her reaction, I pressed my body closer to hers and listened as her breathing became more erratic and shallow while staring at her the whole time. Refusing to back down, she kept her eyes on me until the pressure became too much.

Clearing her throat, she broke eye contact with me and looked down.

"Eh… can you put me down now?"

"I will when you apologize."

"Excuse me?"

"You heard me. As soon as you apologize, I'll let you down."

"You have got to be kidding me?" she asked incredulously.

"Nope, but the choice is yours. I can stand here like this all morning. I have nothing planned until later on tonight."

"Gosh, you're annoying. Fine. Sorry," she said begrudgingly.

"See, now that wasn't so hard." I smiled and placed her back on her feet, but not moving away from her. I liked messing with her. She seemed to get so flustered when she was close to me, but I thought it was cute. This little cat-and-mouse game was fun for now.

"Are we just going to stand here like this or do you want to go eat breakfast?" she asked.

"My fault, go ahead," I said, moving to the side so she could go around to the passenger door.

Getting into the car, I waited until she had on her seatbelt before pulling off towards our destination. The majority of the ride was quiet with us both being caught up in our thoughts until I got tired of the silence.

"So Kylani, tell me about yourself?"

"What do you want to know?" she asked, shifting her body in my direction.

"I don't know. Whatever you want to tell me, I guess. What are your hobbies, dreams, aspirations?" I asked, glancing over in her direction.

"Well, my name is Kylani Vendetti, but my family calls me La. I'm eighteen. I graduate collegiate school in about four months with the second highest GPA in my graduating class. Uh, I wouldn't say I have a hobby, but I like sports and I'm a math geek. I will be enrolling in college for Accounting, but I really want to open a center for single moms to help them with the things the government doesn't help with. School supplies, extra food, household products, things like that."

"Wow, what made you want to do that?" I asked, surprised that a girl that grew up with a silver spoon in her mouth would want to help the underprivileged. I guess there is always more than meets the eye.

"I had a friend back in middle school that was the oldest of five kids and I saw how much they struggled," she answered, shrugging her shoulders.

"Oh, really? Whatever happened to her? Are you two still friends?"

"No, she killed herself our freshman year of high school," she answered and turned her head to look out the window.

"I'm sorry to hear that," I said shaking my head.

"It's okay. I'm over it, but what about you?"

"My name is Orion Alvarez, but everyone calls me Blue. I just turned twenty-two in October. I'm a business man of many talents, but I want to open up a gentlemen's club for the youth," I told her, parking my car.

"Why would you want to open a strip club for minors?"

"I don't. I want to open a club for young boys that are growing up without a father. Teach them what they need to learn to become a man. How to tie their ties, be respected as a man by being articulate and showing them they have more options than running the streets. That's why I called it a gentleman's club," I explained.

By the way she was staring at me, I could tell she judged me from my outside appearance, but I can't blame her because I judged her by what my father told me. I was seeing first hand that he was right, you can't judge a book by its cover.

Over the next hour, we ate our food and got to know each other a little better while joking around. The more she loosened up, I saw her for who she was. Just a normal teenage girl that followed the life that was chosen for her. When we were finished, I drove her back to the park to get her jeep before getting her number and promising to meet her again sometime next week for a rematch in our race. Making sure she got into her car safely, I drove off after she did with my mind and my heart in two different places. I wish the circumstances were different and we would have met at a different point in our lives, but I knew that in a few months, her and her family would be on the front of the Modesto newspaper and I'd be on the first thing back to Georgia. Though that was my only reason for wanting to get close to La, something in the back of my mind told me she would become an important part in my life, but I didn't understand how or why.

Chapter 8: Kylani

Saturday at the park was only the beginning of many days that I spent with Orion. It felt weird if I didn't wake up to a good morning text from him or if I didn't hear his voice after school each day. Exam week came and went and I was beyond excited because that meant I was officially out for Winter break.

August Alsina singing *Kissin On My Tattoos* brought a smile to my face as the song played out because I knew it could only be one person.

"Hello?"

"What's up, baby girl? What you up to?"

Hearing his voice always did something to me. I was never really big on boys and dating, but every time I heard his voice or was in his presence, my center thumped repeatedly until I had to relieve some of its pressure.

"Nothing, about to jump in the shower and just hang out around the house," I replied, plundering through my dresser drawers trying to find something to wear.

"Why don't you hang out with me today? Maybe we can go out somewhere. Besides our weekly runs and talking to you on the phone, I barely get to see you. It's like you not feeling the kid or something," he joked and I could hear the smile in his voice.

"It's not that. I'm just always busy training…" I stopped mid-sentence because I realized I had said too much. Orion didn't know what me and my family were into, and even though he disclosed to me a few weeks ago that he sold drugs, I didn't think he would feel right knowing I was a regular teenage girl during the day, but a robber and jewelry thief at night.

"Training for what?" he inquired.

"Eh, nothing, just this triathlon thing."

"Why you never mentioned it before? I wouldn't mind helping you train when I'm free. I mean, we go running together every other day anyway," he offered.

"No!" I yelled into the phone a little too loud.

"Why not?"

"I mean… I wouldn't want to take up any more of your time than I already do," I said, trying to cover up my last statement.

The sound of someone knocking on my room door saved me temporarily.

"Hey, La. Dad wants us to come down to his office," Amari said, sticking his head in my room.

"Alright. Does he need me right now or do I have time to jump in the shower?" I asked. Even though I needed to take a shower, I wanted to wrap up my conversation with Orion first.

"Dad ain't gone' mind waiting, but mom and Rylan in there too so the choice is yours," he replied before leaving my room and closing the door behind him.

"Hello?" I said into the phone.

"Yea, I'm still here."

"Ummm… what time were you trying to go out? It looks like my dad needs me for the rest of the morning, but I should be free sometime later maybe around five."

"Five works. I got some running around to do with Zane, but I should be free by then. Look, I know you gotta go so I'll text you when I make it in the house. Talk to you later, baby girl."

"Okay, bye." As soon as the words left my mouth, I heard the phone click. I wish I could tell him everything and he would understand, but it wasn't that simple.

* * * *

Every word that my dad spoke went through one ear and out the other. Smiling down at the text Orion had just sent me, I wrecked my brain trying to figure out where he could be taking me.

Orion: Wear something comfortable and some sneakers. Meet me at our spot at 7.

"Kylani, did you hear me?" my dad asked, bringing me out of my thoughts.

"I'm sorry. What did you say?" I asked, putting my phone in my pocket.

"I said we're moving the heist up instead of waiting. I know how much school means to you, so I want to do it the day after your graduation. Here are the maps you'll need," he explained, handing me the papers.

52

"Where is the drop off location for the cash since we'll be a whole town over?"

"Since you're driving the getaway car, I'll let you choose. You need to let me know the day of so I can have a van waiting for you somewhere along that route and you can dump the truck."

Nodding my head, I studied over it for a few minutes making sure I made mental notes of everything before handing them back to him.

"Okay, I got it. I will text you the exact coordinates when I ride out there later on to check things out. I think I can figure it out in five and a half months. So that's definitely enough time. Plus, I'll need that time to practice. I haven't driven backwards in a long time," I chuckled.

"Don't you think you should look that over again? You could mess up the whole plan if you were to take the wrong road," my mom's voice cut through the air.

"No. I already have the only map I need," I replied, pointing to my temple.

"Leave her alone, Leilani. When has she ever messed up a plan? Why do you think I would let her be one of the most important assets on this team if I thought she would fuck up?" my dad bellowed.

"You can't always save her, Kye! And you want her to run this Family? Please, she can't even stand up to me for Christ's sake! She'll never be more than a little girl wanting to play grown up games. The little bitch will never amount to anything more than being a fucking daddy's girl!"

"ENOUGH! I give you passes off the strength that you are my wife and the mother of my children, but you will not disrespect her in my presence!"

"It's okay, daddy. I'm used to it by now. I learned a long time ago that I can't make her love me," I said, getting up to walk out the room.

"See, there she goes running away like she always does! You might as well hand everything over to Amari."

"Yea dad, maybe she's right. I don't think La can handle it either..." Amari started to say.

"Oh, but you can? You can run this family with no fuck ups? You can think rationally and stop being impulsive, right?"

"Yes, I can. You sitting here making it seem like all I do is fuck up. You put her on a pedestal when it should be me you're praising. Your precious La doesn't even want this lifestyle, and she's been saying that the first chance she gets she leaving us far behind. All I hear is how smart she is, but she isn't even Valedictorian of her graduating class, but guess who was? Me!" he yelled, getting hype.

"And do you remember why La let her grades drop? She spent a week in the hospital after you fucked up a jewel heist! She took a bullet in the thigh for you, but she never once threw it in your face that she's had to bail you out time and time again because of your erratic behavior. Every time something goes wrong, La takes the blame so you won't get in trouble, but you're ready to throw her through the mud every chance you get. Quit letting your mom make you feel like you're entitled to something that I built! Nobody built this shit but me! If I want to hand it over to the fucking Pope, then that's my fucking prerogative!"

"Hey, y'all really need to calm down," I spoke up, looking around the room at everybody.

A look of shame flashed through Amari's eyes because I had heard everything he said. I never knew he held that much resentment against me when it came to this business thing and the relationship I had with dad, but I guess it's true what they say, people show their true feelings when they're upset.

"La."

I held my hand up to cut him off, he had already said enough.

"Don't, Amari," I told him. I shook my head and walked out of the room.

My heart hurt in a way I had never felt before. I felt betrayed more than anything because I knew my mom didn't like me, but to know that my brother, the only other man I looked up to other than my dad secretly despised everything about me, crushed my spirit.

"La! La, wait up!" my dad yelled after me.

Wiping the lone tear that had escaped from my eye, I turned around and plastered a fake smile on my face.

"Don't let what they said get to you." He rubbed my shoulder trying to reassure me.

"I'm not. Hey look, I'm going out with a friend for a little while. Don't wait up, I'll be home later," I replied, walking away to my room before he could reply.

Grabbing my phone out of my pocket, I dialed the only person I could think of to make me feel better. I just hoped he answered my call.

Chapter 9: Blue

Kylani calling me crying and asking me to meet her somewhere threw me for a loop. I was caught up handling business with Zane that I couldn't put on hold, so I told her where my spare key was and that I'd be there as soon as I could. That was almost two hours ago. The sun had just gone down, and I was headed to see what was wrong with her.

Pulling up to my apartment complex, I made sure I had everything before getting out my car and headed towards my three-bedroom townhouse. When I walked in the door, I could have sworn that I walked into the wrong one because the smell of food smacked me in the face and one of the most angelic voices I had ever heard serenaded me to follow it.

Following the voice into my kitchen, I watched Kylani as she prepared two plates before turning around to stick the utensils she was using into the dish water, all while giving Ariana Grande a run for her money as she sang her hit song *Best Mistake.*

She sang her heart out as she moved around the kitchen like she lived there with me and I couldn't help the trance she had me in. I didn't want to interrupt her because she seemed in her element, but whatever she cooked had my stomach begging for some.

"I didn't know you could sing," I stated, making my presence known to her.

"Dammit, Blue! You scared me!" she said, grabbing her chest.

"Oh, so I'm Blue now?" I smirked, eyeing her. Since the moment I had met her, she had been calling me by my government. No one ever did, not even my aunt and dad, so I kind of got use to her saying it.

"Yes, you're Blue when you're getting on my nerves."

"Mhm, whatever you say, ma. What you cook?" I asked, walking over to the stove to look in the pots.

"No, sir. Go wash your hands, I already fixed your plate. I was about to put it in the oven because I didn't know how long you would be. It'll be waiting for you when you get back." She dismissed me with a point of her finger.

I stared at the back of her head for a few seconds in amazement before leaving to do what I was told and sure enough, when I came back she had my plate on the table with a glass of green tea beside it. Taking my seat at the table, I was more than ready to dig in. Baby girl had done the damn thing with a plate full of grilled chicken breasts, homemade cream potatoes, corn on the cob and corn bread.

As good as it looked, I waited until she had fixed her plate and joined me at the table to say grace before devouring my plate. We ate in silence for a few minutes. The only thing that could be heard was our forks hitting our plates and the soft music playing in the background.

"I hope you don't mind. I kind of figured you would be hungry when you got in for the night," she said, breaking the silence.

"Na, I don't mind. I appreciate it. I haven't had a home cooked meal since I got here. I normally cook for myself, but I've been trying to establish my own spots up here since I never have time to cook. I usually just grab something and come home to crash. So, thank you."

"You're welcome. I'm glad I could help," she smiled softly before finishing up her plate.

When we both finished our meal, she got up to clean the kitchen. I watched her move around just taking in her presence and trying to figure out my infatuation with this girl. Everything was just supposed to be business, but baby girl had me gone in a month's time. I knew I was feeling her for real when she called me crying and I was ready to turn the whole city inside out. I wasn't too big on affection so I never allowed myself to get into those situations, but baby girl was surely changing that about me.

When she came over to pick up my plate, I pulled her down on my lap and wrapped my one of my arms around her waist to hold her in place.

"So, are you going to tell me why you were crying earlier?" I asked, brushing a piece of her hair out of her face.

"It's nothing too serious. I just got into it with my brother and my mom," she replied, fidgeting with her fingernails.

"Do you want to talk about it?"

"No, not really."

I knew her mom was a touchy subject for her. She had told me one day while we were running about the relationship she had with her family. Apparently, the relationship with her mom had always been rocky, but she spoke so highly of her dad and brother. So, for her to say that she got into it with her brother, I could understand why she was hurt. I didn't have siblings, but I looked at Zane as the closest thing to one I would ever have.

"Okay, we don't have to talk about it. So, what do you want to do?"

"I'm not ready to go home just yet. Is it okay if I hang out here with you?" she asked, looking up for the first time since I sat her on me.

"Yea, I'm cool with that, but hop up so I can get in the shower," I told her, tapping her thigh lightly for her to stand up.

"Okay, I'll finish cleaning up in here and then I'll wait for you in the living room."

"Alright, that's cool. Find a movie too. Oh yea, there's some throw blankets in the hallway," I told her, pointing toward the hall closet as I made my way out of the kitchen.

"Kay."

It took me close to fifteen minutes to get showered. When I got out, I dried my body off and threw on some sweatpants. I didn't bother putting on a shirt or boxers since I slept naked. It made it easier for me because when she left all I had to do was take them off and crawl into bed.

Making it to the living room, I saw that she had made herself comfortable. She must have brought a bag with extra clothes because she had changed into this PINK! lime green and black shorts and sports bra set with the matching socks. Making sure that all my doors were locked and my alarm was set, I walked back towards the living room and flopped down on the couch beside her.

"What we watching?"

"Belly."

"Girl, what you know about Belly?" I joked.

"Boy please, Tommy was that nigga!" she laughed.

"Let me find out you a little hood."

"Whatever, this is one of my favorite movies. Now shut up so I can watch the movie."

As we watched the movie, I pulled her feet onto my lap and tried to get as comfortable as I could without invading too much of her personal space. Close to the end of the movie, I looked over and saw she had fallen asleep. Trying my best not to wake her, I took her feet off my lap and scooped her in my arms and made my way into my room. Laying her down as gently as I could, I turned around to leave without making too much noise.

"You don't have to leave. I really should be going. I didn't realize it was so late," she said, stifling a yawn.

"You can crash here. I can sleep in the guest bedroom down the hall. Plus, you don't need to be leaving out this late by yourself.

Even though this is a gated complex, I don't know them well enough to put anything past them."

"Are you sure?"

"Yea, it's cool. Get some rest," I told her, closing the door on my way out.

As soon as I made it to the guest bedroom, I stripped down and got into the bed. Within minutes I was down for the count. I wasn't sure how long I was asleep before the dipping of the bed beside me woke me up.

"I didn't mean to wake you. I just didn't want to sleep alone," she said, pulling the cover back.

I attempted to stop her before she could move it completely, but it was too late. My dick sprang to life as soon as she pushed the sheet back. It was dark, but there was just enough moonlight in the room for her to see my full length.

"I'm sorry!" she yelled, trying to pry her eyes away, but every few seconds she would steal glances at it.

Chuckling lightly, I reached over into the dresser drawer beside me and grabbed some briefs to slide on. When I had put my piece away, I tugged lightly on her arm, pulled her down on the bed with me and wrapped my arm around her waist before dozing off to sleep.

* * * *

When I woke up the next morning, Kylani was no longer beside me. Glancing over at the alarm clock on the night stand, I saw that it was a quarter to nine. Dragging myself out of bed, I handled my personal hygiene before going to look for her. Before I could make it to my room, she rounded the corner headed toward the kitchen.

"Good morning," she smiled, pushing her hair out of her face.

"Morning. Where you headed?"

"I was getting ready to head home. I got a text from my dad. He isn't too happy that I stayed out all night. Besides, I didn't want to overstay my welcome any more than I already have."

"Who says you're bothering me?" I eyed her. "Besides, you owe me a date. I'll let you go smooth over things with your family because I know you need the peace after everything that happened last night, but meet me back here in two hours."

"Are you asking me or are you telling me?"

"Both. Let's be clear though, ma. I can never MAKE you do anything. All I can do is tell you what I want and give you the chance to decide for yourself. With that being said, let me retract my previous statement. I want the chance to make up the date that I had planned last night. You in or na?"

When she didn't answer right away, I headed to the kitchen to fix a glass of orange juice and grab a muffin. I could feel her eyes follow me with every move I made, but I decided to ignore her until she answered my question.

Jumping up on the island, I faced her so she could see she had my undivided attention as I took slow sips of my orange juice.

"Well…?" I probed.

"I think you're bipolar," she answered with a straight face.

The look on her face was so serious all I could do was laugh as I tried to decipher what was going on in her head.

"And why would you think that?"

"Because your moods change with the tick of a clock. The day after we met, you basically kidnapped me and threw me in your car. Now you're telling me that you can't make me do anything. You're the living reincarnation of Dr. Jekyll and Mr. Hyde," she giggled.

"I wouldn't say I'm bipolar. I just know I can control some situations and others I can't. This is one situation I can't control. If you walk out that door and decide you don't want to come back, it's not like I can kidnap you and make you go on a date with me. That choice is yours." I shrugged my shoulders and finished eating my muffin.

"Uh-huh. Well, I won't make any promises. Depending on how this goes over with my parents will depend on whether I can go later. I can let you know in the next hour."

"Fair enough. Let me walk you to your truck."

"Okay."

Placing my cup in the sink, I hopped off the counter and made my way to where she was waiting by the front door. She was still struggling to keep her curls out of her eyes, and the look of annoyance on face made her look like a little girl.

Ushering her out the door, we walked caught up in our own thoughts. I could tell she was nervous about going home because she checked her cell phone at least four times in the past minute.

"What are your plans for your Winter Break?" I asked her once we made it to her truck.

"I don't have any. Guess I'll be staying in the house and studying these next two weeks."

"You know Christmas is next Thursday, so I'll be leaving Monday headed back to Georgia. I may be gone until the New Year, but I haven't figured it out yet."

"Oh, I see. Well, I hope you have fun on your trip."

I wasn't sure what possessed me to say the next words that flew out of my mouth, but I swear it was like word vomit.

"Why don't you come with me?"

"Huh?"

"Come to Georgia with me. You gone' be here bored by yourself and besides, you're moving there this summer anyway. Why not come kick it with me in my neck of the woods?"

"I can't. Thank you for the offer, though. Have fun with your family and I'll see you when you get back. I should be going. I'll text you when I can confirm our plans for this afternoon."

"Ight. Be safe." I kissed her on her forehead and opened the door for her to get inside before closing the door behind her.

Sticking my hand in the pockets of my sweats, I waited for her to pull out of the parking spot before I made my way back into my townhouse.

"What was she doing here?" I heard someone say from behind me.

"Why the hell you always appearing out of thin air like you trying to be the next Houdini or some shit? Better be glad I ain't have Jet'aime or I would have shot yo' dumb ass."

"Move around with that fuck shit. Back to my question, what was she doing here so early?" Zane asked again.

"Not that it's any of your business, but she stayed the night here last night," I answered, making my way through the front door.

"You fucking up. Why does she know where you lay your head at in the first place?"

"Damn, nigga. Are we fucking?" I spun around and gave this nigga the look of death.

"Don't try me with that gay shit, nigga. You know just as well as I that you fucked up by bringing her over here." He waved me off.

66

"Well, I invited her to Georgia with us too," I told him as I walked back to my room.

"Tell me you lying, Blue."

When I didn't respond, he had his answer. Closing the door on the rant I knew was coming, I grabbed everything I needed for my shower and made my way to the bathroom.

"Blue. You my day one and I'd go to war with you, but you diggin' a hole the size of Texas for yourself. When you can't climb your way back out, don't say I didn't warn you."

I knew he only wanted what was best for me, but I had my situation with Kylani under control. I wasn't sure if I was trying to convince myself or him, but either way it went I knew he was right. Nothing could prepare me for the road I was getting ready to take.

Chapter 10: Kylani

Running to Orion was the only thought that popped in my head when shit hit the fan with my mom and Amari. I had learned to never let the things that my mom said affect me, but the words that left Amari's mouth rocked me to the core. There was so much hate and animosity in them, all I could do was shake my head and walk away from him before he saw the tears threatening to escape.

Even though my friendship with Orion was new, I felt safe running to him because he was the only person other than my family that I talked to. Ever since Nicole killed herself, I found it hard to open up to people. She was the only person who knew the real me and the things my family was into, and she never judged me.

Easing my car into its spot behind my dad's Phantom, I grabbed my duffle bag and made my way in the house. I had already text my dad last night and told him I was staying over a friend's, but I knew that whenever I laid eyes on Leilani she would be on that good bullshit. She always was.

My foot wasn't even over the threshold good before I was being knocked back out the door.

"Oh, so you're grown now, huh?"

Grabbing my stinging eye, I could feel the cut her ring had caused. I had been slapped more times than I could count, but this bitch actually punched me in my eye. I had never wanted to lay her out so bad in my life. Biting my lip to keep myself calm, I counted backwards from one hundred and I knew that if I opened my mouth I would just make the situation worse than it already was.

"You don't hear me talking to you?" she screamed at the top of her lungs before drawing her fist back to hit me while I was still on the floor.

Bracing myself for the impact, I closed my eyes but the hit never came.

"What the fuck is going on in here?" my dad's voice roared through the corridor.

Standing to my feet, I brushed myself off and grabbed my duffle bag off the floor.

"Kylani, what happened to your eye?"

"Ask your wife," I replied, keeping my eyes on my mom the whole time.

"What the hell is wrong with you, Leilani? Why the hell did you hit her?" he questioned, accessing the damage done to my face.

"This was the last straw, Kye. She can't stay here anymore."

"What do you mean I can't stay here anymore?" I grimaced as my dad touched my broken skin.

"Exactly what I said. You are no longer welcome in my house."

"Now hold on a minute, Leilani..." my dad started to say.

"No dad, it's cool."

"You're eighteen, La. You can't stay out on your own."

"Yes, she can. I won't tolerate any more blatant disrespect from her."

"Me? Disrespect you? Bitch, when have I ever disrespected you?"

"Kylani, now wait a minute. You're out of line. I know you're upset, but she's still your mother."

"When has she ever cared that she's my mother? Huh? Tell me one time where she acknowledged that I was her child or thought about the bullshit she lets fly out of her mouth whenever she says some slick shit to me? I have always respected that she was my mother. That's why the bitch is still breathing!"

"Are you threatening me, little girl?" she seethed, her eyes forming into slits.

"We don't make those remember? I'm simply stating facts." I gave her ass a Kanye shrug.

I was furious on the inside and I won't say I wasn't a little hurt, but I wouldn't let her see that she had finally broken me.

"You have five seconds to get the hell out of my house before I forget that I birthed you."

The laugh that left my lips didn't even sound human. I probably looked deranged at this point, but I had to laugh to keep from crying. Bypassing her, I was making my way upstairs to my room to pack some clothes, when she pulled my hair.

My hand reacted before my brain could tell it to stop. I punched her just as hard as she punched me, laying her out with one hit. I shook my head at her before taking the steps two at a time.

"Kylani!" I could tell in my dad's voice that he was angry that I hit her, but she had it coming.

Blocking out his voice, I walked into my room and locked the door behind me. I laid my suitcase and matching carry-on bag across my bed and went through my dresser drawers and closet throwing as much stuff as I would need in them. It took me close to fifteen minutes to get everything together. Going to the safe that I kept in the back of my walk-in closet, I put in the code and grabbed out enough money I felt would last me for three months.

Zipping up my bags, I grabbed the luggage and my backpack and was headed out the door. The first face I saw when I made it to the top of the stairs was my dad. Ignoring the look of hurt and disappointment on his face, I kept walking down the stairs and out the front door. As I loaded my bags in the trunk of my Jeep, I could feel his eyes on me the entire time.

"La. Where do you think you're going?"

"I'm sorry, dad. I can't do it anymore. You know just as well as me that there is no turning back from this. Even if I did stay, she'd just make my life a living hell. I'll be okay, I promise." I gave him a weak smile. "I know you don't understand, but I need to do this." I tried to reassure myself more than him.

"Here," he told me, handing me a ring of keys.

"What are these to?"

"That's to a condo downtown that I've had for the past six months. I had planned to leave your mom, but I never got around to leaving. I'll feel better if you stayed here instead of out in the streets."

"Thanks, dad." I kissed him on the cheek before walking around to the driver's side of my car.

I watched as he blew me a kiss and walked back into the house. All the tears I had been holding in since I walked in the house came pouring out as I broke down and cried from the very depths of my soul. I cried for every hateful word she ever said to me, every decision that was made for me, and everything I could never cry about before. I wasn't sure how long I sat in my truck crying, but when I was all cried out I started the engine and pulled out into the street and decided that was my last time crying over my mom and her ways. I didn't know what the future held for me, I just knew I couldn't keep being the weak Kylani anymore.

Chapter 11: Amari

I hadn't seen La since the argument she had with our mom and that was almost three days ago. I was gone when she came home the next day and my mom said that she kicked her out. The shit I said about La was out of line and I didn't think that she would end up getting kicked out because of an argument, but my dad was convinced that she was safe so I just had to trust him on that.

Christmas was in two days and it would be weird not having La around, but if she wanted to stay away over a petty disagreement then that was on her. Rylan, my mom and I had been working on perfecting the heist without La. Just in case she doesn't show.

I loved La to death, but her flaking on this heist could be my blessing in disguise. Most of the time I needed her, but I was determined to pull this off without a hitch. I would be the next head of the Vendetti Crime Family even if it killed me.

"Have you heard from Kylani?" Rylan's voice asked from behind me.

"Nah. I called her earlier and she sent me to voicemail. I guess she's still salty about what went down," I replied, shrugging my shoulders.

"You really hurt her feelings, bro. You know La idolizes you and for you to say some hateful shit like that had to cut her deep. Have you tried to apologize?"

"Apologize for what? The truth? I'm sorry she had to hear it, but I meant everything I said. La isn't built right to run the family business. Hell, my dad didn't let my mom run the Family, no matter how much of an asset she was to him. It's not for women. If it was up to me, I'd just take the shit by force," I vented, saying the last part under my breath.

Thinking of overthrowing my dad was the ultimate taboo and even though I trusted Rylan, I couldn't chance what I said getting back to him.

"Are you sure that's what you want?" he questioned, giving me a look I couldn't quite read.

"Am I sure of what?"

"Of what you said? Are you sure you want to overthrow your dad?"

"I mean. If I could yea, but that would take an army that I don't have and no offense, me and you couldn't do it alone."

"I know we couldn't, but I know someone who can." The smile he had on his face made me uneasy, but against my better judgment, I asked anyway.

"Who?"

"Your mom."

I wasn't sure what he meant by my mom, but apparently he knew something I didn't and I was more than ready to find out.

Chapter 12: Blue

The plane ride back to Georgia was a long one, and I had never been so happy to see the state of Georgia in all my life. I missed home something serious and I was ready to get this assignment over with so I could come home to stay.

The pilot had just announced that we would be landing within the next twenty minutes. Those words were like music to my ears. Glancing over to my left, I noticed that La was still sleeping. She looked so peaceful even with the cut under her eye. She still hadn't gone into detail about what happened when she got home. She called me over to her place that same day and when I arrived, I was more curious than ever.

Baby Girl: Something came up. Can you come over to see me instead?

I was in my living room chopping it up with Zane when the text came through on my phone.

"Aye. I know you ain't ignoring me?" Zane sucked his teeth when he noticed I wasn't paying attention.

"Nah. It ain't even like that. I just got a text from La asking me to come over her place," I explained as I responded to her message.

Me: Text me the address.

"Over to her people's crib?"

Before I could respond, she had sent over the address and I knew for a fact that wasn't the address of her parent's house.

"Nah. Ride with me?"

"Yeen' even have to ask," he nodded, grabbing his Beretta from underneath the couch cushion.

I hit her back and let her know I was on my way. Grabbing my nine, I tucked it in the small of my back and we were on our way. I didn't see Kylani as the set up type, but you could never be too sure.

After about thirty minutes, we pulled up to a complex downtown. Stepping out of my car, I scanned my surroundings before making my way to the apartment number she had given me. Ringing the doorbell, I checked my gun while I waited for her to come to the door.

Getting impatient, I rang the doorbell again before tapping on it with my gun. It didn't take long before she came to the door with a towel wrapped around her body. Any other time I would have been checking her out, but the cut under her eye had me zeroed in on her face.

"What happened to your eye?" I asked, pushing my way past her with Zane right behind me.

"Sure Orion, you can come in."

"Whatever. What happened to your eye? Better yet, go put on some clothes first and then come back."

"Yes, sir," she replied sarcastically.

Checking out the rest of the apartment, we went room by room making sure no one else was here. The place was already furnished with a black, white and charcoal grey color scheme. In total there were three bedrooms and two bathrooms. The kitchen was laid with stainless steel appliances and a breakfast bar.

Ten minutes later, La walked out of the master bedroom in an oversize Nike t-Shirt that read *"Do It"* on the front and a towel wrapped around her hair. Sitting down on the sectional in the living room, Zane followed suit as I waited for her to explain what we were doing here.

"Whose spot is this?" I asked, looking around at the black and white paintings on the wall.

"Mine now. Apparently it was my dad's, but he gave it to me."

"Care to share with the class why?" I asked, bringing my eyes to meet hers.

"Not really. You're so rude. Hi, my name is Kylani, but you can call me La," she introduced herself to Zane, reaching her hand out to shake his.

"Zane," he replied before shooting daggers at me.

"Nice to meet you. Y'all want something to drink?"

"Nah, not really. But check it, give me your keys. I'm about to hit it. I need to get my car from your house and meet up with this

chick I met," Zane claimed, standing up from the couch with his hand out.

"Alright. I'll just have La drop me back off at home," I told him, placing the keys in his waiting hand.

"Bet. It was nice meeting you, La." He hit her with the head nod and left before she could acknowledge what he said.

"He seems like a bundle of joy to be around," La said once she had locked up after him.

"Don't take it personal, ma. He just don't know you. So, are you going to tell me what's going on or did you call me over here to stare at my handsome face?"

"There's nothing to tell."

"What happened to your eye?" I questioned.

"Nothing I can't handle. I didn't know if you still wanted to go out or not, so I invited you over here," she said, changing the subject.

I nodded my head. I let it go for now, but I didn't like secrets. One way or another, she'd eventually tell me.

"Yea. Go change into something comfortable. Oh, and make sure you wear sneakers."

"Where we going?" she asked, standing up from the spot she had been occupying on the couch.

"To play laser tag."

The smile she gave me was like a little kid in a candy store. Without another word, she took off down the hall full speed to get dressed. For the rest of the night, we kicked it and the subject of what went down at her house didn't come back up, but I could tell I was a much needed distraction.

Arriving at my aunt's house, I could see that the whole family was already there. Grabbing the luggage out the trunk, I waited for La to get out the car before walking side by side in the house.

"Did you tell your aunt you were bringing me?"

"Nah. She won't mind though. She's always telling me I need to bring a girl home to meet her." I smirked down at her nervousness.

"It's so much colder here than in Cali."

"Ain't nobody to tell you to dress half naked with your stomach out. I told you to dress for the weather change."

"How was I supposed to know it would be this cold if I've never been outside the state of California?" she countered, giving me the evil eye.

"Is that my baby?" I heard my aunt say.

Taking my eyes away from La, I saw my aunt standing in the doorway. Smiling at her, I made my way up the steps to give her a hug. My aunt was my heart in human form. I'd lay down and die for her.

"Hey, auntie," I greeted, kissing her on the cheek.

"Who's your friend?" she asked, looking past me.

"Auntie, this is Kylani. Kylani, this is my aunt Mia," I pointed, making the introductions.

"It's nice to meet you, ma'am."

"No need to be so formal, sweetie. You can call me Mia or just auntie. You're a very beautiful girl."

"Thank you," La smiled.

"Zane, show Kylani where to take her bags. And don't make me slap you for coming to my house and not speaking to me," she snapped, shooting daggers at him.

"My fault. You looking beautiful as ever," he replied, kissing her on the cheek.

"Yea, whatever. Now go do what I told you." She waved him off.

"Yes, ma'am."

When they had made it out of ear shot, she turned around and looked at me for a long time and I knew she was trying to read me.

"Say it, Auntie."

"I like her. She has a good vibe to her."

"How can you tell that and she didn't say more than twenty words to you?" I questioned, raising my eyebrow at her.

"I can tell."

You would swear that my aunt was way older than she was. She made forty-two look golden and as much as I hated to admit it, she was my mother's twin. They were identical with the butterscotch colored skin, silky black tresses and deep brown eyes.

"Okay, auntie."

"Whatever's wrong with you, it will all be better soon."

"How did you...?" I started to ask before she gave me this knowing look.

Just like when I was younger, she could tell when something was bothering me. Choosing not to respond, I simply nodded my head as we made our way into the house to join everyone else. The rest of the night went off without a hitch. Everyone was getting along, and Zane even made an effort to talk to La on his own. For the first time in weeks, I actually felt at peace, but I had a feeling that this was the calm before the storm. Nothing could prepare me for the tornado that was brewing.

Chapter 13: Kylani

Christmas Day...

This is the first Christmas I've spent away from my family and I wasn't exactly sure how I was supposed to feel. I had been texting my dad on and off since I landed in Georgia, and I was missing them like crazy. Even my mom, but I knew that staying away would be the best thing for me.

Getting my emotions in check, I pulled my hair back into a tight bun before applying ointment to the cut under my eye. Thank God it wouldn't leave a scar. I slid on the cream-colored sweater dress and burgundy thigh-high boots that Ms. Mia had taken me to pick up yesterday evening at the mall. Giving myself the once over in the mirror, I added a light coat of nude lip-gloss to my lips before being interrupted by a faint knock on the door.

"Come in," I called out with my back to the door.

"Good morning." I smelled him before he even opened his mouth. Facing his direction, I smiled shyly.

"Morning. You look very handsome," I complimented.

"You don't look half bad yourself. Even though you jocking the kid's style for the day," he chuckled, leaning against the door frame nudging his chin in my direction.

Glancing back and forth between of us, sure enough we both were wearing cream and burgundy. He wore a cream colored v-neck sweater, some light denim jeans and burgundy loafers. Giggling lightly, all I could do was shake my head.

"I told you that you be stalking me," I teased him, picking up my necklace off the dresser.

"Allow me," he offered, closing the door and walking in my direction.

Handing him the necklace, I put my back to him while watching him secure the necklace in the mirror. The cologne he wore was intoxicating and had my head swimming. Bringing his eyes to meet mine, he reached him arm around the front of my body, lightly brushing his hand against my breasts as he adjusted my necklace. I wasn't wearing a bra, so the sensation of the fabric on my breasts instantly made my nipples hard.

Taking a step closer, I felt his manhood brushing lightly across my butt causing me to close my eyes. I could tell he wasn't hard, but from the size of his bulge I knew he was blessed. Clearing my throat, I tried to get a grip on my hormones as I stepped out of the embrace we were in.

"I think your aunt will be looking for us if we don't get downstairs."

"Yea, you probably right. Come on, scary," he smiled down at me, grabbing my hand in his and guiding me out the room. I was in awe of this house. From the outside to the inside, it was spectacular. Walking through the foyer, I looked at the pictures of Orion that decorated the walls and even the mantle. There were pictures of him winning spelling bees, football tournaments, basketball trophies and even science fairs. One picture that caught my attention was a picture of him as a toddler with a woman that was almost identical to his aunt. The only real difference was the woman was a bit shorter than his aunt and she had deep dimples. He must have noticed me staring at it.

"That's Linda."

"She's beautiful." I smiled up at him.

"Yea, she was." He stared at the picture with a faraway look in his eyes before he abruptly dropped my hand and made his way down the stairs, taking them two at a time.

"Don't take it personal. He doesn't talk about his mom much," I heard Zane say from behind me.

"Is she dead?" I asked, still looking at the picture. In the picture, they looked so happy and you could see the love she had for him in her eyes.

"To him, she is," was his reply as he walked past me and made his way downstairs.

I wasn't exactly sure what he meant by that. Whenever we were together I would always talk to him about my family, but he barely mentioned anyone other than his aunt and on a few occasions he brought up his dad. Deciding to drop the prying thoughts, I turned away from the picture and went to meet up with everyone else.

Stepping into the kitchen, I swear it smelled like heaven. I had never seen or smelled something so delicious. Ms. Mia had gone all out with scrambled cheese eggs, grits, biscuits with gravy, bacon, sausage, white rice, pancakes, cinnamon roll waffles, and fresh squeezed orange juice. I heard people from the south loved to cook, but she had really outdone herself.

"Good morning, baby. I was wondering where you were when I saw my big-head nephew walk in here without you."

"Oh, I got caught up marveling over his pictures in the foyer. I guess he got tired of me staring," I giggled as I made my way over to the table to join everyone else.

"He was a cute kid, wasn't he? I don't know what happened as he got older," she joked.

"Whatever, auntie. You know what they say, I'm like wine, I get better with time." He gave her his half smile and winked his eye at her.

"Boy, please. More like sour milk."

I couldn't help the laugh that erupted from my stomach as I tried to keep myself from spitting out my orange juice. Over the course of breakfast, they had a playful banter back and forth. If you didn't know any better, you would swear they were mother and son. I sort of envied their relationship, but at the same time I was happy to witness how much love his aunt held for him and Zane. On the strength of how much she loved them, she showed me the same affection and it felt amazing.

After breakfast, more of his family started to show up. His uncle Kane, his wife Carmen and their children. I was literally being pulled in every other direction by his aunt as she introduced me to everyone. By the time everyone was ready to open presents, I was more than ready to sneak away so they could have their family time.

Slipping out the front door, I sat on the swing on the porch and thought about everything that led me to today. I was so completely wrapped up in my thoughts that I didn't hear anyone walking up the driveway until she was almost to the steps. Thinking my eyes were playing tricks on me, I did a double take as I eyed the woman from the picture.

"Hi. I was wondering if Mia was home?" she spoke in a raspy voice.

"Umm, yes. She's inside with everyone else."

"Oh, okay. Why aren't you inside with everyone else if you don't mind my asking?"

"Oh, they were having family time and I didn't want to feel like I was intruding."

"This is your first Christmas with the family?" she asked.

"Well, sort of. I came with a friend of mine," I explained.

"I see."

"Aren't you going inside?" I questioned, trying to figure out why she was standing out in the cold with me.

"I guess I'm sort of like you. I don't want to intrude on their family time," she answered, taking a seat next to me on the swing.

"I don't think you would be bothering them. This is your family, right?"

"Yea, but I haven't seen them in years and the last time I did wasn't so pleasant. I'm not sure if they'd want to see me."

"Where are my manners? You're listening to me ramble on but I didn't even bother to introduce myself. My name is Linda." She reached her hand out.

"Nice to meet you. You can call me La." I shook her awaiting hand. A few seconds later, the front door flew open.

"La, what are you doing out here…?" Before he could finish his question, his eyes landed on Ms. Linda. His face went from worry, to curiosity and confusion to rage in a matter of seconds.

"Why are you here?" he seethed.

His tone was so cold that the shit hurt my feelings, like he was talking to me. I had never seen him this upset. Either he was being an asshole or he was joking around. The look in his eyes was murderous and the way Linda was opening and closing her mouth, I could tell she wasn't expecting his reaction.

"She was just…" The look he shot in my direction snatched all the words out my throat.

"Go in the house, Kylani."

"But I…"

"GO IN THE HOUSE KYLANI! NOW!"

Slightly jumping out of my skin, I hurried to my feet and made my way inside the house. I wasn't sure what this woman had done to him, but it must have been bad. Scurrying in the house, I went to grab Ms. Mia before he did something he would regret. I just hoped I made it to her in time.

Chapter 14: Blue

Twenty minutes into opening presents, I realized that Kylani wasn't around to open any of the presents that Zane and me picked out for her while she was out shopping with my aunt last night. Thinking she probably went to the bathroom or something, I combed the whole house for her. When I came up empty, I went outside. Imagine my surprise when I found her on the front porch holding a conversation with the female that birthed me. As much as I had no love for her in my heart, she was still the reason I walked the Earth so I'd never disrespect her by calling her a bitch.

"Why are you here?" I repeated my question when Kylani had run in the house, leaving the front door wide open.

"I came here to see my sister," she answered while looking me over from head to toe. The smile of accomplishment on her face pissed me off in a matter of seconds and I couldn't understand what she needed to see Auntie Mia for when she hadn't shown her face since she abandoned me.

"You've grown to be so handsome. I remember how tall and lanky you were as a kid. You swore you'd be skinny forever and that no girl would ever like you." She chuckled at the memory like it was the funniest thing she had heard in years.

"Don't do that."

"Do what?"

"Reminisce. It'll save me and you a lot of trouble. Now again, why are you here? You need money to feed your habit or let me guess, you're here to steal something else? What is it, huh?"

"How dare you? You don't know shit about me and what I've been through!"

"I know that you're the same junkie that left her son on her sister's front porch in only a thin t-shirt and jeans to chase your next high. I know that you're the same one that came back around when I was thirteen-years-old and stole auntie's flat screen TV and her jewelry for a measly two hundred dollars. I also know that you are the same one I caught on the side of the corner store sucking off a local corner boy's dick to feed that nasty monkey on your back. So nah, I think I know you pretty well. In my line of business, we call those type of people crackheads."

I felt the slap before my mouth could close again from the words that I spoke, but the slap didn't come from Linda. It was my aunt who was standing next to me with tears in her eyes and a look of pain etched across her face.

"Orion, I raised you better than that. Apologize to your mama."

"I don't have a mama. My mama died when I was seven," I replied, keeping my eyes locked on Linda as I spoke. Those words must have hurt more than anything I said to her before. Watching the tears well up in her eyes, I turned around to walk away before I could see them fall.

Making my way in the house, I could hear my aunt yelling at me to come back and apologize, but I just couldn't. No one understood how I felt at this moment. Slamming the door shut to my old bedroom, I flopped down on the bed and stared holes into the ceiling. I knew I would have to apologize to my aunt later about my behavior, but I would wait until I calmed down to face her.

The slight creek of my bedroom door opening alerted me that someone was in the room with me. Smelling her Etc! perfume before she made it over to my bed calmed my nerves a little. Without saying a word, she took off her boots and climbed in the bed beside me mimicking my pose. We laid like that for a good thirty minutes before I rolled on my side to face her.

"Are you okay?" she whispered, tracing her finger across the tattoo underneath my left eye.

"Yea, I'm straight baby girl."

"Do you want to talk about it?"

"Nah, not for real. The shit depressing as fuck, for real."

"I've noticed."

"Oh yea, why'd you run off earlier when we were openin' Christmas presents? You didn't get a chance to see the gifts I got you."

"You bought me something for Christmas?" she asked, sitting up on her elbows to look at me.

"Yea. Was I not supposed to?"

"No, it's not that. I just didn't expect you to. Thanks," she blushed.

"Yea, yea," I teased, tugging on her bun she had on the top of her head.

"Ouch. Blue, that hurt!" she whined, smacking my hand.

Keeping my grip on her hair, I flipped over and pinned her arms down underneath my legs as I took out the ponytail holder she had in her hair.

"What are you doing?"

"Stop before I body slam you," I warned.

"You wouldn't dare," she said, squinting her eyes up at me.

In one quick motion, I slid my body down hers, grabbed her arm and her leg and threw her over my shoulder as I stood.

"Now what was that?"

"You better not, Blue."

"Say I won't again and I'll show you better than I can tell you."

"You won't!"

She thought I was playing with her. Tossing her onto the bed like she was a sack of potatoes caused her hair to fall into her face as she looked at me like a lioness stalking her prey. If looks could kill, I would have fallen dead where I stood. No lie, the way she was staring at me had my shit on brick and I was ready to put this dick in her life.

"You're an asshole. You know that?"

"You said it so it must be true," I smirked at her before flopping back on top of her.

"Get off of me. You're heavy," she groaned, wiggling underneath my weight.

"Nah, I think I'm good." I laughed at the look on her face.

Next thing I knew, she started to tickle me and I lost all my damn marbles. Imagine tickling a 250lb man and him giggling like a fucking school girl.

"Alright, man. I quit! I quit!"

"Awh. You're ticklish," she laughed, tickling me again.

"Stop man!" I laughed, jumping out the bed onto the floor.

"What's wrong with being ticklish?" she asked when she caught her breath from laughing at me.

"I'm too damn big to be ticklish. That shit is embarrassing as fuck. What grown ass man you know that's ticklish?" I questioned.

"You."

The look on my face must have been hilarious because she fell out into a fit of giggles. I could do nothing but laugh too.

"But foreal, one of the other reasons I hate getting tickled is because it makes my dick hard."

"How does getting tickled make your dick hard?"

"I'on know." I shrugged my shoulders.

Now it was my turn to laugh because the way her eyes bulged out of her head was funny as fuck. She was trying her hardest not to look to see if I was really hard or not. Allowing my eyes to roam over her body, I noticed that her dress must've come up while we were play fighting because the palms of her cheeks were playing peek-a-boo with me.

Feeling my dick get hard, I tried to focus on everything else, but the shit was hard. I could tell by the look in her eyes that she was curious, but I wasn't trying to take it there with her, even though I wanted to.

"Let me go downstairs to talk to my aunt Mia and then we can go open your presents."

"Okay, that's cool. And thank you for inviting me. It really has helped me keep my mind off all my drama," she said smiling at me.

"No problem," I told her, getting up off the floor and heading out the room to smooth things over with my aunt.

The rest of my Christmas went off without a hitch. My aunt ripped me a new one for the shit I said to my mom, but she had to understand where I was coming from. Before going to bed that night, my aunt handed me a letter that my mom gave to her for me hoping I would read it. I wasn't sure I was ready to read it, but when I was I would see what she had to say.

* * * *

Waking up the next morning my mind was clouded with thoughts of seeing moms. On one hand I wanted to hate her, but I couldn't deny that I missed her. I had been walking around with all this anger and resentment towards her. I felt like when I needed her the most she wasn't there for me. In a way that's why I loved my dad as hard as I did because he was the only parent I had even though he wasn't a model citizen himself.

The conversations I had with La and my aunt kept sounding in my head telling me to hear what she had to say, and to give her a chance to explain why she left. The nagging thought in the back of my head brought my mind to the letter that my aunt handed me last night. Seeing it sitting on the night stand beside the bed, I threw my legs over the edge of the bed and sat up to grab it. I had to stare at the cursive writing of my name on the outside of it for a good ten minutes before I got the courage to open it and see what it said. There were only five words on the paper along with an address, a phone number and a time, but those words alone spoke so much volume.

Beware of those around you.

Checking the time, I saw that I had a little over three hours to make it to my destination and it would take me a minimum of thirty minutes to drive out there. Jumping out the bed to handle my hygiene, I decided that today was an all-black kind of day. Grabbing some black cargos, black on black timberlands and a black thermal out of my closet, I got what I needed for my shower and headed to the hallway bathroom.

Stepping into the hallway, I tried to be as quiet as possible trying my hardest not to wake anyone. It was still pretty early and I knew my aunt wouldn't be waking up for the next hour or so. Before heading to the bathroom, I went to check on baby girl. Thinking she was asleep, I didn't bother to knock and walked in on the highlight of my day. Kylani was sitting on the bed in a towel rubbing body butter all over her smooth ebony skin. I probably seemed like a creep for real, but every time I was around her I got caught in this trance and all I could do was give her my undivided attention.

"You know, I'm starting to think you're a stalker for real." Her soft voice sliced through my thoughts and made me clear my throat.

Damn. What the hell is wrong with me? She's just some girl. A young girl at that.

I wasn't sure what it was, but I found myself standing directly in front of her. I had been trying to avoid taking it there with her, but a nigga couldn't fight it no more.

"What are you doing?" I could hear the nervousness in her voice, but I didn't bother answering her as I pushed her back on the bed and opened up her towel. I hadn't really paid much attention to it before, but baby girl had a quarter sized scar on her right thigh close to her pelvic bone. Bending forward, I trailed kisses from her knee up to the scar and did the same thing on the other leg.

Her center had the sweetest smell to it and without thinking twice, I dived in head first. Swirling my tongue around her clit, I gazed up to see the look of pure bliss on her face. Adding a little more pressure, she started squirming uncontrollably, causing me to put a death grip on her thighs to hold her in place.

"What… what are you doing to me?" she moaned out, closing her eyes shut tight.

"Open your eyes, La."

Seeing that her eyes were still closed tight, I stopped my assault on her pussy and sat up on my elbows, keeping my weight on her thighs.

"Why did you stop?" she asked, looking down at me breathing heavy.

"Because you didn't do what I asked. Keep your eyes on mine the whole time. If you close your eyes, I will stop. Understand?" I questioned, running my tongue along the inside of her thighs.

Nodding her head, she kept her eyes on mine as I licked the wetness dripping from her folds. Laying my tongue flat, I licked from her clit to her crack and back again. Stiffening my tongue, I tried to stick it in her while I strummed her clit. Keeping my thumb on her clit, I kissed up her body, paying close attention to her navel and each of her breasts. When I tried to stick my fingers inside her to see if she was ready, I felt like I had ran into a brick wall. The way her whole body tensed, I already knew what the issue was.

"Are you a virgin?" I asked, looking into her eyes.

"Yes."

"Damn," I cursed underneath my breath as I removed my body from on top of hers.

"No. I want to."

"Are you sure?"

"Yes."

Getting off the bed, I pulled down my briefs and gauged her reaction as my dick sprang to life. It was only semi-hard, but the more I stroked it the more it lived up to its full potential. The way her eyes bulged out of her head, you'd think she seen a ghost. Walking out the room back to my room with the towel she was using wrapped around my waist, I rummaged through my dresser drawer until I found what I was looking for. Placing the Magnum on my dick, I grabbed the bottle of water based lube before returning to the room. The look in her eyes almost made me want to change my mind about taking her virginity. I had heard the horror stories about how crazy chicks get when you pop their cherry, and Lord knows I don't need any more stress or drama in my life. But, the look of wanting and hunger in her eyes cancelled out any second guessing I had going on.

Climbing between her legs, I rubbed some of the lube on the tip of the condom and made sure she was wet enough so I could slide in her without too much added discomfort. Placing her arms in the crook of my arms, I placed my dick at her opening before laying my body on top of hers.

"You sure you want to do this, ma? You can stop at any time, you know that right?" I questioned, making sure she understood I wasn't trying to pressure her into anything.

"I want to."

"Okay. Now this will hurt... a lot," I told her before placing my lips on top of hers and pushing my way inside of her.

"Owwwww."

Her muffled screams and the way she dug her nails into my back had my dick about to go soft. Pushing the rest of myself inside her, I sat still for a moment to get her used to my size. When her breathing had relaxed a little, I rocked slowly in and out of her.

"It hurts," she groaned, clamping her eyes shut.

"I know, baby. Just relax, it'll get better," I said, kissing away the few tears that had escaped. I licked and kissed on her neck, trying to add some pleasure somewhere so she wouldn't focus on the pain between her legs.

After a few minutes, her whimpers turned into full blown moans as I picked up my pace.

"Blueeee."

"Damn." Every time I pulled out, her walls gripped my shit and pulled me back in. I had to keep reminding myself that this was her first time so I wouldn't start wilding out in her shit, but when she started to circle her hips, that was all she wrote.

Pushing her feet towards the headboard, I watched as my dick moved in and out of her until I felt her walls put me in a death grip.

"Move. I have to pee," she moaned, pushing me back.

"No, you don't. Nut on that dick, ma," I groaned, pushing her legs further back.

"I can'ttttttt."

"Yes, you can. Let it go."

Feeling her pussy pulsing against my dick, I watched the look of ecstasy on her face before pulling my dick out to the tip and slamming back inside of her until she squirted all over my dick, thighs and sheets. After a few more strokes, I couldn't hold out much longer. Pulling out, I released in the condom. My pull out game is a beast, but I wasn't taking any chances. Falling back on the bed, I completely forgot that I was at my aunt's house and I'm pretty sure her moans woke the whole house.

"Hey, I gotta make a run out somewhere, but when I get back we can go out and do something. Cool?" I asked, looking over at her.

"Yeah. That's fine," she mumbled with her eyes closed. I knew I had worked her little ass out, but I didn't expect her to fall asleep. Kissing her on the forehead, I climbed out of bed and headed to take my shower. I had killed at least an hour out so I needed to wake Zane up and bounce so I could see what my mom had to say. I just hoped that whatever she said didn't have me questioning everything.

Chapter 15: Kylani

My relationship with Orion had grown over the past few months. The week with him and his aunt was a definite change for me. After losing my virginity to him, we developed this bond and I found myself with him more and more. Even though he was busy keeping order in the streets, he took time out of his schedule to at least spend one day with me with no distractions. If we didn't kick it at one of our places, then we went out on dates like paint-balling, riding four wheelers, and even just shooting basketball.

I had yet to go back to my parents' house, but we had started to talk more and I even went back to training for the heist we had coming up. Regardless of my feelings for my mom, my dad had a lot riding on us pulling off this job so I tolerated everything she threw my way.

I had about three weeks left before graduation and I was just trying to get through these exams. My last one was today and it was for my math class. After this, I was free of homework for at least two weeks before I started my summer classes. An hour later, I had aced my exam and was officially done with my senior year of high school. I stopped by my locker to make sure it was empty before making my way into the senior only parking lot. Replying to the text that Orion had sent me, I declined his offer to take me out for dinner. As much as I wanted to go, I needed to train for this job in a few weeks.

"Well, how about lunch then?" I heard him say.

Tearing my eyes away from my phone, my eyes landed on him leaning against his car and a smile spread a mile wide across my face. I swear, this man was the definition of fine. With his cargo shorts, collared t-shirt, Sperry's and fitted Polo hat, he was killing the thuggish-preppy look. He was the only one I knew that could pull the attire off with so much ease.

"Where you thinking?" I asked when I was standing directly in front of him.

"I'm in the mood for some Steak N Shake. What you think?" he asked, brushing a curl from in front of my face. I knew how much he loved my hair in its natural state, so I rarely pulled it up into a ponytail anymore unless I was running or training.

"Real burgers and hand stirred shakes. Hell yeah, I'm in," I laughed.

"You silly, ma," he laughed with me, pulling me close to him by the belt loops of my jeans. Standing on my tip-toes, I kissed him lightly on the lips. Deepening the kiss, he ran his fingers through my hair pulling my face closer to his. His lips were so intoxicating and every time we kissed behind closed doors, it turned into him teaching me something new that I didn't know about myself. In a matter of five months, I had turned into his personal sex kitten. He taught me things about my body and showed me how to please him.

"Aight, that's enough. Let's go before we end up skipping lunch altogether and back at my apartment or something," he groaned, breaking the kiss.

"You driving," he told me, tossing me his keys.

That's one of the things I loved about Orion. Things with him were simple, and in a way he had become my best friend. He always made me feel safe and I knew that if I had no one else in my corner he would be right there rocking with me. More than ever I was ready to get this training over with so I could focus on being the girl he thinks I am. I wasn't ready for him to learn the true Kylani. I knew he would leave me high and dry and I prayed I could hide it a little while longer, but even I knew that was wishful thinking.

Chapter 16: Kylani

Graduation Day…

There was so much tension between me, my mom and Amari that I avoided them altogether, but with it being graduation night I had to be on my best behavior. My mom was so fake. All she cared about was appearances and looking like she had her shit together in front of everyone, but if they knew just how phony and evil the bitch was they wouldn't think twice.

Removing the thoughts from the back of my mind, I checked my appearance in the mirror to make sure my hair was in place and my dress was fine for after my graduation dinner.

"La, are you almost ready to go? Dig just pulled the car up front and dad's waiting on us," Amari asked, sticking his head in my room.

I had just slipped into my cream-colored blazer and was giving myself the once over. The nude color heels that I paired with the halter, navy-blue dress matched perfectly with it.

"Yea, I just have to grab my purse and my cap and gown to put in the car," I told him, turning away from the mirror once I was satisfied with my appearance.

"Let me grab that for you." He reached over and took the bag from my hand.

"Thanks." There was an awkward silence that fell between us as we made our way downstairs.

"So, did you prepare your speech?" he questioned, breaking the silence.

"It's not really a speech. It's just a thank you, I guess. You know I'm not big on talking to people I don't know."

"You'll have to grow out of that eventually. You won't be around me to talk to like that too much longer with you leaving later on this summer and all. Spelman, right?"

"How did you know?"

"I saw the letter in your room. Why didn't you tell me?"

"It's not set in stone. I promised dad I would give this training my all and that's what I'm doing." I wasn't sure how I felt about him snooping around my room while I wasn't home. I made a mental note to start locking my room when I left the house.

"I think it would be a good opportunity for you to explore life outside of California. I know how much you don't want to live this life and this is your chance to do just that. Just tell dad you want me to run the family business instead."

Here goes this bullshit. I don't know what was up with him and my mom thinking I would just tell my dad I didn't want to do it. In the beginning that was true, but now I wasn't sure how I felt. On one hand I wanted to go off to college, but the other part of me had a point to prove. I had to show them that I was more than they thought. I didn't even respond to what he said because it wasn't worth the wasted air I would release from my lungs. He was our mother's child. If it wasn't his way, it was the equivalent of beating a dead horse and I didn't have time.

* * * *

The ceremony went by faster than I expected. After I gave my speech, it was over. Walking through the crowd of people in search of my family, I wasn't paying attention to where I was going and ran into someone, almost losing balance in the four-inch heels that graced my feet.

"Damn, baby girl. Just because I knocked you over when we first met doesn't mean you gotta do the same thing," Orion joked, catching me before I could fall.

Smiling up at him, I was at a loss for words. I had mentioned it a few days ago when I was at his house that I had graduation tonight, but I wasn't expecting him to come. I would be lying if I said I wasn't excited to see him though.

"What are you doing here?" I asked, sliding out of his embrace and giving him the once over.

The three-piece black on black Armani suit he wore gave him a sophisticated look that had me drooling. Hearing someone clear their throat caused me to look over to my left. Meeting the eyes of Zane, I gave him a quick nod of approval. I had never noticed before, but Zane was actually cute. He was light skin, tall with sandy colored hair that he kept cut in a curly taper, almond-shaped brown eyes and a goatee trimmed to perfection. The white suit he had on fit him to a tee.

"Hey, Zane," I greeted, smiling up at him.

"What's up, La?" he replied, giving me a simple head nod.

The look of annoyance he gave Orion didn't go unnoticed and I swore they were having some kind of silent conversation that I wasn't in on. Orion must have seen me staring and shook his head discreetly at Zane, but I saw it. I made a mental note to ask him about that later, but for now I would let it go.

"But to answer your question, I came to see you graduate. I wouldn't miss it for anything in the world."

Opening my mouth to answer, I was cut off by my dad's voice.

"That was a great speech. I am so proud of you," he smiled, pulling me into a hug.

"Thank you, daddy."

"Who are your friends?" he questioned just as my mom, Amari and Rylan walked up.

"Oh. Daddy, this is Orion and this is his friend, Zane. Guys, this is my father, Kye, my mother, Leilani, my brother, Amari and you met Rylan already."

"You look familiar, Orion. Do I know you?"

"No, sir. I don't think you do."

"I may know your family."

"Nah. I don't think you do. I'm not from around here. I actually have only been living here for two months now. I'm originally from Georgia."

"That would explain the accent. Well, it was nice meeting you both. La, we'll be in the car waiting for you. We have a reservation to make in thirty minutes."

"Okay, daddy. I'll be right there."

Turning back around to say my goodbyes, there was this look Zane was giving Orion that I couldn't quite read. I had always been good at reading people's body language. He looked completely unbothered on the outside, but the way his breathing suddenly changed told me something else.

"Your father seems like a great man."

"He is. Well, I have to go. Call you when I make it home?"

"Sure," he said, kissing me on the top of my forehead and following behind Zane as they made their way towards the back exit of the auditorium. Staring at them until they were out of sight, this feeling washed over me telling me that the little exchange they had meant more than what it seemed. I just didn't know how much more until it was too late.

Chapter 17: Zane

"Man, what the hell was that?" I asked as soon he closed the passenger door on my Dodge Charger.

"What you mean?" he feigned ignorance.

"You too close to this. I think this has a lot more to do with just a job. You feeling that girl a little too much."

"Who, La? Man, it ain't even that deep. Baby girl is a job. No more, no less." He waved me off before checking his phone. I wasn't sure if he was trying to convince me or himself, but I wasn't buying it.

Blue had never been the type to let a girl cloud his judgment and make him lose sight of what he supposed to be doing, but I could see it in his eyes when he looked at ol' girl that she had his mind gone.

Damn, I'm rude as hell. Let me introduce myself. My name is Zane and I'm twenty-one years old. I met Blue after he moved into my neighborhood with his aunt. Some kids from around the way were talking about his mom being a crack whore and I swear all hell broke loose.

"I'm telling y'all, his mom was behind my apartment building giving my uncle head for a twenty rock. That shit was looking so good that I almost asked if I can join!" this boy Jordan laughed, dapping up his little minions that flocked around him like he was the best thing since all-white K-Swiss.

"My mama ain't no crack whore. Take it back!"

That was the first time I had heard him say more than two words unless a teacher was asking him a question in class.

"Or you'll what?" he challenged, getting up in Blue's face.

Before the words could leave his mouth good, Blue pounced on him and gave him the business. When I saw one of Jordan's home boys jump into the mix, I started swinging too. Wasn't no jumping around my way. If he could talk shit, then he should have been able to back that shit up. From that day on, we were joined at the hip. If you saw me then he wasn't too hard to find and vice versa.

"Aye, nigga! You don't hear me talking to you?" Blue yelled, snapping his fingers in my face.

"Man, what?"

"I was asking what Tech say about that shipment that was supposed to come in later on today?"

"He said that everything should be ready by eight. Are you riding out with me or are we driving your car?" I asked, glancing over in his direction. The smile this nigga had on his face could light an abyss. I swear he was showing all thirty-two, but instead of calling him out on it, I let it go. Whatever baby girl was saying in them text messages had that nigga happy as hell.

"Uh… we can drive your car," he replied after he put his phone back in his pocket.

"Alright. Well, we can ride over there now. We already dressed for the occasion anyway."

Even though the stay in Cali was supposed to be temporary, there was nothing wrong with expanding your business to somewhere you frequented often. Hell, I was always down to make more money.

"Aye, my dad just called me. Swing by the compound really quick and let's see what he wants. He says it's important."

Nodding my head, I followed his instructions. We had about thirty minutes to make it to this meeting, so I hope he makes this quick. Pulling up to Blanco's mini mansion, we saw him outside the door waiting for us with a cigar in his mouth and what I assumed was a cup of Bacardi in his hand.

Throwing the car in park, we got out and met him half way. I never told Blue how I felt, but even though I respected Blanco off the strength that he was my right hand's pop, I never trusted him. When he first put us on this mission to bring the Vendetti's down, I was for it because we were getting paid half a mil a piece when it was finished, but at the same time, the story didn't add up. I know Blue had his suspicions too, he just didn't voice them. If I know Blue the way I think that I do, he will go with the flow until he feels some static and then he would act on them.

"What was so important that you stopped me from going to my meeting to swing by here?" Blue asked once we were in ear shot.

"You two look like you headed to a party or something."

"That's neither here nor there. We on pressed time."

"There is going to be a drop tomorrow off of old county road headed out of Modesto that I need you two to get for me. These are some new cats around the way that say they want to get some product. I don't know them, so I want you to go check everything out and make sure they have all my money. If everything pans out, the product will be a little over half a mile away in a white van parked on the side of the road close to the camp grounds," he explained, taking a sip from his cup.

The hairs on the back of my neck stood up immediately and I'm guessing that Blue felt the same way too because I saw him when he shot a look at me from the corner of his eye.

"Why you not sending Bullet and Piranha like you always do? They're the muscle for a reason right?" I asked, lifting my eyebrow.

"They will be busy doing something else for me. Is there a reason you two can't do it?" he questioned, looking me in the eyes.

Tightening my jaw, I counted backwards from ten in my head to calm myself. I had to remind myself that he was basically my boss, but he was testing my gangster at this moment. Smiling through my anger, I threw my hands up in surrender and kept my mouth closed because I wasn't sure what would come out.

People mistook my pretty boy features and laid back demeanor as me being bitch-made, but I was far from it. I was the type to break your neck at the dinner table then resume my meal as if there wasn't a dead body sitting there. I wasn't crazy or nothing, I just didn't tolerate disrespect.

"Just text me the time and we'll be there. Let's go Zane, we about to be late for this meeting," Blue said, pulling on my arm as he walked in the other direction.

Finally taking my eyes off of Blanco, I followed behind him but I kept my eyes on Blanco. The nigga's whole aura screamed "bitch nigga" and the moment he got out of line, boss or not, I was pushing that nigga's shit back. No questions asked.

Chapter 18: The Phone Call

Ring. Ring. Ring

"Hello?" the voice on the other end of the phone answered.

"I have a mission for you and your team."

"And what would that be?"

"There is an armored truck that will be passing through US 99 leaving Modesto headed North bound on Friday at three p.m. There will be approximately twenty bags in the back with 200,000 dollars in each. I told you I would eventually need that favor that you owe me and now is that time."

"Are you sure you want to waste your one favor on a robbery?" the voice questioned from the other side.

"Yes, I'm sure, but make sure your people are packing just in case something goes wrong."

"That's a must."

"Okay. I will send you more information no later than Thursday night with the coordinates. Tell your people to be ready, they only have one shot at this. No witnesses and hit everything moving if the time comes. I want that money."

"Understood," the voice confirmed before releasing the phone call.

Chapter 19: Amari

Today was the day of the truck heist and I was ready to prove to my dad that I was fit to run the business. The tension in the house over the past few days had been so thick you needed a machete to cut through it. I apologized to Kylani about the shit she heard that night and even though she said she forgave me. She was still acting funny. Plus, she was barely around now that she moved out and I believe it had something to do with the dude Orion she introduced us to last night at her graduation.

Rylan told me later on that night that he was the same dude he saw her with at the park, but he introduced himself as Blue at the time. He looked a little rough around the edges, but if he was keeping La distracted from taking over the family business then he was okay in my book.

We had about an hour before we had to head out and we were going over some last minute details, making sure that everything was ready to go. My mom had pulled me to the side earlier and told me that if everything went as planned that I would be taking over the family business sooner than I thought. Hearing that had me hyped and I was ready to get this over with.

Once we went over the final details, La gave our dad the coordinates over where we would meet up with him once we finished since she would be driving the van as our getaway vehicle. As we drove, I tried to pick La's brain to see where her head was at.

"So, what's going on with you and the guy that you introduced us to last night?" I asked through the small window of the back of the truck as she drove.

"Who, Orion?"

"Yea. Rylan mentioned that he saw you two in the park together running a few months back."

"Rylan needs to mind his business for one and two, he's just a friend. I told Ry that the day he saw us."

"He looks more than just a friend to me."

"Well, that's your problem not mine. Amari, focus. There's the truck right there," she said, pointing ahead of her.

Looking over the side of the truck, I could see the Loomis money truck about six car lengths in front of us. Glancing down at my watch, I saw that we were right on schedule. Placing the ear piece in my ear, I gave her the signal and held on tight as she slung the truck around and drove backwards behind the truck.

"Rylan, open the door!" I yelled into my mic while I tried to balance myself.

Not even twenty seconds later, the doors to the truck opened up and I was met by Ry in his work uniform.

"Aww, don't you look cute," I joked as I jumped in the back with him.

"Nigga, fuck you," he shot back, flicking me off.

"Guys, focus! We only have three minutes," La's voice came through the earpiece.

"Alright, alright."

Grabbing two bags at a time, we threw as many bags as we could into the cab of the truck before the people in the front realized something wasn't right. We had eight bags in the back of the truck, which was more than we originally planned.

"Come on. We got it, let's go!" Ry said, pulling on my shoulder.

"Jump! I'm right behind you."

Ry jumped on the back of the truck and told La to keep the truck steady so I could jump across. Glancing over my shoulder, I saw that there were four more bags on the floor of the truck and the opportunity was too good to pass up so I grabbed those as well.

"Amari, what are you doing man? We have to go now!"

Before I could open my mouth to answer, shots rang out. The shots must have scared the driver because next thing I know I was being thrown all around the back of the truck. Gaining my balance, I held on to the bag that was in my hand and started to make a running jump back to the truck La was driving.

As soon as my body was visible, the sound of automatic rounds pierced the air.

Rat. Tat. Tat. Rat. Tat. Tat.

A sharp pain shot through my leg as I was jumping. When I was safely in the back of the truck, I lifted my head to see two people dressed in all-black on the back of two sleek, black and red Ducati motorcycles toting AK-47s.

"Is he in?" Kylani screamed as she returned fire while trying to keep the pickup from veering off the road.

"Yea, I'm in! Let's go!" I yelled, picking up my custom plated Beretta and returning fire.

"Hold on."

The truck came to a screeching halt as she threw the truck in neutral before hitting a U-turn and driving back in the opposite direction from where the shooters were headed. Bullets were flying from all sides and I cursed myself out for not bringing a bigger gun.

Rounding the corner, I saw the van waiting for us and I breathed a sigh of relief, but that was short lived when the truck swerved off the side of the road and ran into a tree. Dazed, I looked up to see the two motorcyclists hopping off their bikes headed in our direction.

Looking inside of the truck, I could see blood dripping down La's forehead and all over the front of her shirt. Drifting in and out of consciousness, the last thing I remember was the passenger door of the truck being pulled open and someone carrying La's body away from the truck before more shots rang out. Then it was lights out.

Chapter 20: Blue

"Pops!" I yelled, storming through the living room of my dad's place. On everything I loved, I was ready to rip his head off his shoulders. One thing I hated more than a thief was a liar, and he lied in my face without so much as blinking an eye. If you can tell a small lie then you can tell big ones and that was a serious no-no in my book.

"Aye, Pop!"

"Why are you walking in my house yelling like you lost your mind?" he questioned, coming into view from the kitchen.

"What the fuck was that? That wasn't no fucking drop off. As soon as we rounded the corner, shots rang out! You could have got us killed and for what?" I was so heated spit flew with every word I spoke and my face was beet red.

"Calm down, son."

"How the hell am I supposed to calm down when you sent me into some shit blind when you didn't have to? What was the point in lying about a drop when you could have just told us that you wanted us to air a motherfucka out? All you had to do was say the word and it would have been done! I hate a motherfuckin' snake and you moving real slimy right now, my G."

"Watch how you talk to me and in mi shit. Um still yu father and yu will not disrespect me in mi shit." His accent was coming through so I knew he was getting mad, and any other moment I would have heeded the underlying threat in his voice, but this wasn't one of those times. All I could see flashing through my head was all the blood dripping down La's face and not knowing if she was okay was fucking with me. I was checking on her when bullets started to fly and we had to book it before the cops showed up.

I had been calling her since the moment I left and I wasn't getting an answer to any of my calls or text messages. In that moment, I realized that my feelings for her were deeper than I thought they were. I wouldn't be able to live with myself if something happened to her and it was my fault.

"Why does it even matter that mi sent yu into something blind? If dey start shootin' then yu shoot back. It's dat simple."

I couldn't believe the shit that was coming out of his mouth right now. What the hell does he mean "what did it matter?" Of course the shit mattered. The person standing in front of me wasn't the same man I looked up to during my adolescent years and some of my adult years. I didn't know who this person was.

Zane stood off in the corner just watching everything unfold and by the look in his eyes, I could tell he had some shit he wanted to get off his chest too, but he was trying his hardest to bite his tongue.

"Keep biting your tongue Zane and you're gone' end up biting that motherfucka off. Speak your peace," I told him, unzipping the jacket to my biker's outfit.

"How did you know that they were gone' be there?"

"What did you say?" I questioned, bringing my eyes up to meet his.

"Think about it, Blue. That shit they had going on looked like an inside job. They weren't worried about us, they were trying to rob a damn armored truck. So my question is, how did he know they were gone' be there?"

Before he had completed his sentence, the wheels in my head started to spin. I hadn't even given it much thought, but it was strange that he knew La and her family was robbing that truck and sent us. As if a light bulb went off in my head, I realized that he had to be working with someone in her family.

"You're overstepping yur boundaries here, Zane." My dad spoke with calmness in his voice that I found odd. He basically just got caught playing both sides of the fence, but he wasn't the least bit nervous or angry.

"Answer his question, pop."

"If yu knew de answer, would it change yur mind at all from what yur tinkin' bout mi?" he questioned, looking me square in the eyes as he spoke.

Thinking over his question, I came up with the answer in less than a few seconds, but I just stared at him trying to figure out his angle.

"No, it wouldn't," I finally answered, never breaking eye contact.

"Then der is no point in mi tellin' yu." He shrugged his shoulders and walked off like he was dismissing me altogether.

"I never thought of you as a snake, but it's true what they say. Even snakes don't give a fuck about family," I chuckled.

"Yu don't want mi as your enemy, Orion."

"Are you threatening me, nigga?"

"Yu know mi well enough to know I don't make dos.'"

"Bet," was the only thing I said as I made my way out the house with no intentions on looking back.

I had to get to La and explain everything to her before my dad got to her. If someone in her family was working with him, it was only a matter of time before she got touched and I couldn't have that on my conscious. I said a quick prayer to God that once she found out the truth about why I approached her, she would find it in her heart to forgive me, but even I knew that was asking a lot.

Chapter 21: Kylani

"What the hell happened?"

"I don't know... we were loading the truck, and then suddenly shots rang out. Kylani tried to dodge the shots, but we ended up going into a tree."

The raised voices in the room were making my head hurt worse than it already did. Sitting up from the laying position I was in, the room spun and I felt as if my head would split into two at any second. Closing my eyes tight, I tried to gather myself to keep the room from spinning.

"What I'm not understanding is, who the hell would try to do a hit in broad daylight?" I could finally make out my dad's voice.

"Calm down, Kye. It's not their fault," my mom told him.

"How do you expect me to calm down and my daughter is in there with a gash in her forehead and a bullet hole in her shoulder?"

"Why is it that every time something happens involving all of them, you find a way to make it about your precious Kylani?" The disgust in her voice couldn't be hidden.

I had heard enough at this point and I was just ready to get out of here. I didn't have time for her attitude.

"I'm fine," I said, finally letting them know I was awake.

"Hey baby girl, how you feeling?" my dad asked, rushing over to where I was.

"My head hurts, but I'll make it."

"Can you stand up?"

"I think so."

Trying to stand up the first time was unsuccessful, but after two more attempts I stood up without an issue.

"I think you may have a slight concussion. You have a pretty nasty cut on your forehead that needed ten stitches and the bullet was removed from your left shoulder. We couldn't risk taking you to the hospital. so we had someone come over and patch you up," my dad explained.

"I'll be okay. How long have I been out?"

"Since yesterday."

"Dammit. Do you know where my phone is?" I asked, looking around the room.

I was supposed to meet Blue today for our date and by this point he's probably feeling some type of way.

"It's in your room," Amari answered.

Walking to my room as fast as the pain would allow me, I spotted my phone on my dresser when I walked in. Seeing that it was dead, I put it on the charger and hopped in the shower. Looking myself in the mirror for the first time, I saw that my forehead was a little bruised where the stitches were and my lip was busted, but other that I was fine. My shoulder was killing me, but with pain killers and this sling hopefully it would ease some of the pain.

Stripping out of my clothes, I adjusted the water and hopped in. Avoiding getting any soap and water on my bullet wound, I let the shower rinse all the dirt and grime off my body as thoughts consumed my mind. This was the second time I've been shot within the last year and I was just thankful that I walked away with my life.

Wrapping a towel around my body, I waltzed into my room in search of something comfortable to wear. After I decided on a PINK! Jogging suit, I pulled my hair back with a band as best I could with one hand and applied some Neosporin to my lip and forehead. It was a struggle putting my clothes on with one good arm, but I managed. Securing my arm in the sling, I was ready to go.

I grabbed my phone, powered it back and waited for it to come to life. Before the screen could come on good, my phone started to vibrate out of control. There were over fifty text messages, my voicemail was full and at least sixty missed calls. I knew they could only be from Blue, so I dialed his number and waited for him to answer.

"Damn ma, that's how we doing it now? I gotta blow up your spot for you to call me back?"

"It's not even like that. I just got caught up yesterday and my phone died," I responded, downplaying the situation.

"Mm-hmm. I need to talk to you about something. Can you meet me at Steak-N-Shake in about thirty?"

I didn't want him to see me in this state, but it would be weeks before I healed so I might as well get it over with now.

Throwing caution to the wind, I agreed to meet up with him and we talked a little more before disconnecting the call. I wasn't exactly sure how I would explain the busted lip and the gash, but I would think of something.

Pulling in the parking lot of Steak-N-Shake, I saw him posted on the side of his Malibu waiting for me. Giving myself the once over, I applied a little Carmex to my lips and hopped out to meet him halfway.

"It's about time. I told you to be here in thirty minutes, not an hour."

"I know. I got caught up talking to my dad."

"Tell me anything, ma. So, what do you want…" he paused in the middle of his sentence and I already knew what had caught his attention.

"Yo, what happened to your forehead and why is your arm in a sling?" he asked, grabbing my chin and tilting my head from side to side to assess the damage.

"It's nothing, I was running up the stairs in my socks and lost my balance and hit my head on one of the steps and dislocated my shoulder," I told him, pulling my chin from his hands.

For a few seconds he just glared at me and I don't know why, but I felt as if he knew I was lying.

"Is that your final answer?" he questioned in a low tone.

"Yes, it's my final answer because it's the truth."

"You something else ma, you know that?" he chuckled, running his hand over his mouth.

"What's that supposed to mean?"

"It means that I hate liars. I came here to keep it a buck with you and you sit here and lie in my face like I ain't shit to you. People only lie when they don't trust someone with the truth."

"How are you going to tell me that I'm lying?" I asked, offended.

"Because I was there!" he snapped.

"What do you mean you were there?"

"Just how it sounds. I was there. I know you didn't fall and hit your head. You hit your head, but it sure as hell wasn't on no staircase."

"You're talking in riddles right now. Can you please just say what you got to say?"

"Fuck it. I came here to tell you the truth anyway, so here it goes. I know you didn't fall and hit your head because I watched with my own eyes as the truck lost control and ran into a tree on county road 99 yesterday."

My stomach fell to the pit of my stomach. I heard the words that left his mouth, but I was trying to understand how he could have possibly known.

"How?"

"I know who you are, La. I've known since the moment I approached you. I know that you're one of the youngest jewel thieves and bank robbers on the East coast and I also know that you and your brother are responsible for pulling off a heist a few months back that resulted in you securing over 6.4 million dollars in diamonds."

"Who are you?" I asked, back-tracking towards my truck.

"I'm who I always said I was. I may have never told you the real reason I approached you, but I never lied to you about who I was. I can at least say that I showed you the true me, but that's more than I can say about you, now isn't it?"

"And what reason was that?" Even though I already knew the answer, I asked any way.

"I was sent to kill you and your family, but after getting to know you I couldn't bring myself to do it. I had numerous opportunities to kill you like the day in the park or the night you stayed at my apartment, but I didn't. I kept telling myself that you weren't the person my father painted you to be, but I was wrong. You're no better than him, you're a liar and a thief. I came here with the intentions of telling you the truth and praying that you forgave me, but at this point I no longer care. As long as I warn you, then I've done my part."

"Warn me about what?"

"Someone in your family is working with my family to plot against you."

"And why should I believe you?" I asked him, trying to keep my voice even.

"To be honest with you, I don't care if you do or if you don't. I laid all my cards out on the table about everything else, so why would I lie about this? Like I said before, as long as I warned you then I did my part. Now what you do with the information is up to you, but it's whatever. Have a nice life, Kylani," he said, walking away.

I stood there for a good five minutes after he pulled off and tried to piece together in my mind what just happened. He reveals that he planned to kill me, but gets mad at me for lying to him about what happened to my forehead and arm? This shit was a real eye opener for me. I was tired of the people in my life feeling like they could use me or keep me around for their benefit until they didn't need me anymore, and then throw me away when they wanted. I must have had "pussy" stamped on my forehead. I wasn't sure if I believed Blue or not about what he said about my family, but he had a point. He came clean about everything else, so why lie about that? I didn't know who the person could be, but I planned to find out.

My mom talks to me any way she wants and I hold my tongue off the strength that she was my mother, my brother feels I'm not good enough to run this family when I'm the one that keeps him from getting killed on the regular, and now Blue feels like it's okay to plot against me, tell me the truth, and then walk away as if I was in the wrong the whole time. As of this moment, the old Kylani was dead and gone. I was about to show them the reason my last name was Vendetti. Let the games begin!

Chapter 22: Zane

Ever since the day after the shootout with that girl La's family, Blue had been walking around like he had something shoved up his ass. I swear, that nigga was always mad about something and the littlest situation was bound to make him snap.

The only good part about it was that he had been in the business full force. We were making triple the amount we were when we were in Georgia. Even though Blanco had cut us off for the time being, Blue made a few calls and linked up with this cat down in Florida by the name of Rock. Apparently, this nigga had a connect out in Brazil and everything he was bringing over here was pure.

I was over at the warehouse going over the count with Piranha and Bullet when Blue came through the door toting two duffle bags.

"What's up?" he greeted us before pulling up a chair and emptying the bags on the table with the rest of the money.

"How much is this?" I asked, sifting through the knots of money.

"Kimo says it's supposed to be 70 bands altogether. They even took the time out to band them up for us, but you already know how I feel about that," he said, undoing one of the knots and counting it over.

"Exactly. These little niggas new, so ain't no telling what they gave us," I told him, banding up the cash I had in my hand and dropping it into the duffle bag on the floor beside me.

"Damn, y'all don't trust nobody, huh?" Bullet said laughing.

"We trust y'all, don't we?" I asked, looking between him and Piranha.

"Fair enough," he said, nodding his head before going back to counting the money.

After our fall out with Blanco, Piranha came over to the spot one day and asked could he be down with us. He and Bullet had been friends of ours since we were younger, but they worked underneath Blanco when he needed some muscle and we vouched for them. Bullet had been keeping an eye on Blanco for me since I was suspicious about what he was doing. When everything went down, he gave us all the information he had and we started to plan our next move.

They didn't know who the snake was in Kylani's camp, but they would continue to work underneath Blanco until they figured it out. Blue had told us about him coming clean to her and warning her before he basically walked away from her. I didn't understand him, but then again it wasn't for me to understand. If he likes it, then I love it.

Two hours and fifteen minutes later, we had over 375,000 dollars banded up and ready to go. I placed 250,000 thousand in one duffle for the re-up and the rest was going in the safe we kept at my paint and body shop, *Custom Paint & Body*. Oh, y'all thought I was just some average d-boy, huh? Nah, I'm far from that. Once the others left, me and Blue stayed back and chopped it up, planning our next move.

"So, what's going on with ol' girl?" I asked for the hell of it.

"Man, fuck Kylani," he snapped, sucking his teeth.

"You funny as fuck, you know that?"

"How?"

"How you gone' call yourself getting mad at her for lying to you about how she got the cut on her forehead, but you been lying to her since the moment you opened your mouth?" I questioned, raising my eyebrow.

"That's different," he replied, waving me off.

"No, it's not. A lie is a lie, regardless of how you tell it. You go against the only parent you have for this girl just to turn around and cut her off, all because you in yo' feelings? I don't see why you won't kiss and make up with her already," I told him, shrugging my shoulders.

"It's not that simple."

"You in love with her, so how is it not?"

"Who said I was in love with her?" he inquired with a hint of laughter in his voice.

"Your fucked up ass attitude, that's who. You been on one since the day y'all fell out. Hell, you got me ready to hunt down the bitch just so y'all can make up. If the pussy got you acting like this, then I don't want to meet a bitch that got any of that between her thighs. That shit is lethal. I'll pass."

"Nigga, fuck you," he laughed. "But on the real, don't call her no bitch again," he said once he stopped laughing.

Throwing up my hands in mock surrender, I left it alone because I knew I'd probably feel some type of way about the chick I love. And him saying that further proved my point on why I said he was in love with her.

"You need to get your girl back."

"As I stated before, it's not that simple. The ball's in her court. She gotta learn on her own. I got a deep regard for shorty, but she has to boss up. I can't tolerate lying. If we can both get past the lies that this was based off of, then I'll go to war with God behind her, but she gotta come to me. That's a decision she gotta make for herself."

I could respect what he was saying. I was just ready for them to kiss and make up because I was ready to put our plan into motion. When it was all said and done, heads would roll and me being me, I lived for this type of shit. I knew shit was about to get real and I was more than prepared for the war ahead.

Chapter 23: Blue

I know it seems crazy to most, but I couldn't vibe with La knowing that she sat in my face and lied to me without so much as a second thought. It sounds hypocritical coming from me, but it is what it is. I can't change how I feel. I missed missing baby girl something serious though, so to keep her from roaming around in my mental, I jumped into work full force and that's why I'm swimming in duckets now.

The events over the past few weeks had me on edge with everything I did. I knew my Pops better than most people knew their lovers. He would try to wait it out before he came for me, but he was eventually coming. Knowing him he expected me to be on the first thing back running to Georgia, but I couldn't knowingly leave Kylani in harm's way, even if I wasn't rocking with her like that at the moment. And that alone is why Bullet and Piranha alternated shifts on keeping eyes on her at all times when they weren't with us.

While I sat on the couch throwing shots of Dusse back, the conversation that I had with my mom the day after Christmas came to my mind.

Zane and I had just pulled up to the address that she had put on the letter my aunt gave me. The house was in a cul-de-sac in a quiet little neighborhood. It wasn't anything fancy, but it was nice.

Sitting in the car for a few minutes, I tried to get the nerve to hear her out. Yesterday was the first time I had laid eyes on her in almost 13 years and my emotions were conflicted about it. On one side, I wanted to hate her and all that anger and resentment came up every time someone said her name too loud in my presence and then the other side of me wanted that love from her that I yearned for so much as a kid. Contrary to popular belief, I didn't hate her, I just couldn't allow myself to get too close to her.

Saying fuck it, I finally got out the car with Zane behind me as I made my way up the walkway that lead to the front door. Ringing the doorbell, we waited for about two minutes before she opened the door.

"I didn't think you would come," she said, stepping to the side so we could come in.

"To keep it funky with you, I had my doubts about coming, but your note piqued my interest," I told her, looking around her living room. I was surprised to see baby pictures of myself and some of me at different ages. She even had my graduation picture.

"Why did you want me to meet you here?" I asked, giving her my undivided attention.

"Sit down so we can talk. And Zane, you don't have to be so quiet." She gestured for us to sit down on the sofa across from her.

"No disrespect. I'm just not much of a talker," he responded, keeping his answer simple. Zane trusted no one. He kept quiet because he said when you're always talking you can't hear what's going on around you, so he kept his mouth closed and his eyes and ears open.

"I can respect that. Do you two want anything to drink? I have water and tea in the fridge."

"With all due respect, can you just tell me why I'm here? You said 'Beware of those around you'. What is that supposed to mean? The only person that's always around me is the nigga to my right that you see in front of you, and I can vouch for him and say he was there for me in times that you weren't so I never have to question his motive."

"I've taken the little slick remarks from you because I deserve most of them, but you will not keep disrespecting me. I am still your mother. I pushed you out of my pussy after 14 hours of labor. You will respect my mind."

"A dog can give birth, that doesn't make it a mother."

I didn't even see her stand to her feet, but by the time I did it was too late. The two-piece combo she sent to my face had me dazed and seeing stars. She may have been shorter than me, but those hits were packing some heat behind them.

"I just told you not to disrespect me again. That's the problem with your dumb ass. You always running your pussy lickers. If you would have shut the fuck up I could tell you what I had to say, but no, your ass just keep testing my fucking patience. I brought you in this world and I will damn shol' take you out of it and if you don't believe me, say something else that I don't like," she threatened, standing over me.

Rubbing my jaw, I took heed to her warning and kept my mouth shut. I could see Zane shaking his head and trying to control his laughter out of the corner of my eye, but after thirty seconds, he failed miserably.

"Man, mama a savage," he laughed, nodding his head in approval.

"He'll learn one way or another," she told him taking her seat.

"Now as the note said, you need to be more careful of those you have in your circle and I'm not talking about Zane. Orion, you may not believe me, but your father is not who you think he is. Blanco is a ruthless man and is only driven by his greed. I want to ask you a question and I want to give you me an honest answer." When she realized that I wasn't going to say anything else slick, she continued.

"How did you meet the young lady that was at Tamia's house yesterday?"

I didn't expect her question, but instead of lying I told her the truth.

"I met her running at the park out in California. That's where I was staying the past few months."

"Your dad still stays out in California, right?"

"Yea. What's your point?" I asked, getting annoyed. I wasn't with the twenty-one questions. I was ready for her to get on to what the hell she had to say so I could leave.

"*My point is, I can bet you all the money that was given to me by Carlos to disappear and all the money I have saved up over the years that he told you to pursue that young girl. Am I right?*"

The look on my face must have been all the confirmation she needed because the laugh that escaped her lips threw me for a complete loop.

"*Of course I'm right. He's had this hard on for Kye since he stole Leilani from him back in high school.*"

"*Took her from him? And what do you mean the money he paid you to disappear?*"

"*After you were born, Carlos formed this nasty habit of snorting cocaine. Somewhere along the lines, I began to snort with him. In the beginning it was only a little here and there, but by the time you were three, I was a full blown coke head but I was functioning. I kept a job and you wouldn't know I was doing it unless I told you. Around your 9th birthday, I got a call from Carlos saying he was ready to be a family again and that he wanted me to meet up with him. Me being the hopeless romantic I am, I agreed to meet him. When I made it there, he asked me to help him set up Kye to take over the operation he started. When I refused, he said that if truly loved him I would do anything to please him. Being young, I wanted to prove my love to him, but I knew his motives for wanting to destroy Kye was all wrong. He knew I was still snorting powder, so somewhere during the conversation, he pulled out a baggie of cocaine and we snorted together and had sex. I must have fallen*" asleep because when I woke up he had me tied to the bed posts with a syringe in his hand.

He asked me again if I would help him, but when I refused he injected me with the syringe with what I know as crack. My life then began to spiral out of control as he baited me with the drug and at that point, I would do anything he wanted me to do to get it. The night I left you at your Auntie Mia's house was the night he threatened to kill me and you, but told me that if I took the money and left you he would let us both live. I had enough dirt on him for him to be buried underneath the jail, but he knew I would do anything for you. So, I did one of the hardest things I ever did, I left you and ran. There is not a day that goes by that I haven't regretted my decision, but I was a full blown crack head and I knew that Mia could be something to you that I never was."

By the time she finished telling us the story, she had tears streaming down her face. The regret in her eyes and the pain in her voice told me she was telling the truth. I was trying my hardest to wrap my mind around everything, but two questions kept burning in my brain.

"I only have two questions for you. The first is why not just take the money and take me with you anyway? And the second is how much money did he give you?"

"You may not understand, but one of the hardest things about being a parent is being selfless. I could have taken you with me, but at the risk of you having a fucked up childhood because you had a crack head as a mother, I gave you a life that I knew wasn't *perfect. I knew my sister would never let anything happen to you. And to answer your second question, he gave me 1.5 million," she answered.*

"Damn, that's fucked up," Zane said, shaking his head from side to side.

I may not have agreed with the way she went about the shit, but I respected what she did for me because she was right. Even though I grew up without her in my life, I didn't have a fucked up childhood. Aunt Mia never treated me like I wasn't her child and she showered me with the love of two parents turning me into the man I am today.

For the rest of the morning, me and Zane sat around and chopped it up with my mom as she told us shit about my dad that I didn't know and went a little further into the beef he had with Kye Vendetti. We even told her about everything going on and all she could say was watch my back because Blanco would use anyone's pain as his gain. I just wished I had heeded her warning sooner.

Chapter 24: Amari

I had been second-guessing my decision to overthrow my dad, but after the shit with the truck heist all he seemed to be concerned with was Kylani. I pushed all that to the back of my head and said fuck it. If he didn't give a fuck about me why I should give a fuck about him? My mentality was to eat or be eaten, and I wasn't trying to be anyone's lunch.

We saw less and less of La around the house, but when we did see her it was because she was coming to talk to my dad. Something about the look in her eyes and the way she walked changed. I couldn't explain it, but it seemed like something inside her snapped and she didn't give a fuck about any of us or what happened to us. Before, that would have made me feel some type of way, but now it just justified my drive to get rid of her and my dad. As far as I was concerned, this was just a means to an end. It was either me or her, and without a doubt I was aiming to come out on top. Blood or no blood, the bitch had to go. Simple as that.

To someone else my reasons may not make sense, but in all honesty they don't have to make sense to anyone but me. Can you imagine how it feels to be the only boy in the family, but get treated like the red-headed step-child as if I don't belong? My mom had been telling me that my dad loved La more for as long as I can remember, but as I got older I saw it for myself. I tried to do everything to make him proud of me, but nothing seemed to work. She was always better at everything. If I made a simple bird house, of course my dad would show that recognition, but if La built a bird house he would buy her a pony and throw her a party. It was always like that. No matter what I did, La was better at it.

I had finally started pulling off these heists with Rylan by my side. I had something I could do that she couldn't, and for once he was noticing me and telling me how proud of me he was. That was short lived though. He brought La in on it and I basically just didn't exist anymore. I will admit that I have anger issues and sometimes I act before I think things through completely, but it wasn't my fault I was bipolar. I would control the shit, but I couldn't. I mean, I could take my medicine, but I didn't like how shit made me feel. I was a shell of myself and I couldn't get out of my own head. The shit was horrible. That's why I found me something better.

Snorting the line of cocaine off the coffee table, I laid my head back and let the feeling of euphoria take over me. Hands fumbling with my belt buckle made me open my eyes. Smirking down at Rylan, I allowed him to unleash the beast and give me some of the best head I ever had. Around the time that he introduced me to cocaine was the first time I let him top me off. I wouldn't call us gay or even bisexual, he just knew what I liked. It never went beyond my releasing my seeds down his throat when we were high, but he knew how to relieve the stress I was under.

Closing my eyes, I let him finish me off as I guided his head up and down on the length of my dick. When I felt myself about to bust, I kept his head steady as I nutted. Keeping my eyes closed, I tried to gather myself as he stroked my shit back to life.

"Have you decided on what you're going to do about the offer to overthrow your dad?" he questioned.

"Ssss... Yea. Ima do it," I hissed.

"Good. Well, I need you to do something for me."

"Yea, and what's that?" I asked, peeking at him out of one of my eyes.

"Well..."

Letting him run down the plan that him and my mom came up with, a wicked smile appeared on my lips. The plan was fool proof, and I was more than ready to get the ball rolling.

Chapter 25: Kylani

It had been a few weeks since my fall out with Orion and I had been thinking a lot about the conversation we had. Keeping everyone at arm's length was my best way of dealing with everything. I wasn't sure who was working with Orion's dad, but I had a feeling it was my mother. I just wasn't sure how to tell my dad about my suspicions.

I had plans on telling him this weekend when I went over, but for now I had to make sure I had proof before I told him anything. With the help of Bullet and Piranha, I was looking at leads. You're probably wondering how I know about those two, huh? Well, it really wasn't hard to spot them. Bullet stood 6'4 with skin as black as tar and was built up like the Rock. Piranha wasn't much better. He was 6'5, high yellow and skinny with tattoos on every visible part of his body from the neck down.

I was running my mile at the park when I noticed the car for the third day in a row. Instead of ignoring it like I normally did, I walked to see who was behind the dark tint. I expected the car to drive away, but from my guess that wouldn't have been their style. Both of them just got out and waited for me to make my way over. Once they told me who they were and why they were following me, I asked them to help me. Orion sending them to look out for me showed me he really cared about me and when all this was said and done, hopefully we could get back on track.

I can't front and say I don't love Orion because I do. Hell, I may even be in love with him, but how do you get past lies? Our whole relationship was based on a lie, but it created a bond that I felt could never be broken.

As I sat on the couch of my apartment, thoughts of us and the time we shared consumed my every thought. Swallowing my pride, I slipped my feet into my Jordan slides and snatched my keys off the table as I headed out the door.

* * * *

Gathering up the courage, I saw that it was a little after two in the morning. Lifting my hand to knock, the door opened before I could finish the gesture.

Looking into the eyes of a beautiful, brown skin female with a short haircut and deep brown eyes, I took my time looking her up and down. I give props when they were due and baby girl was definitely a looker, but she didn't seem like she would be Orion's type.

"Can I help you?" she questioned in a high pitched voice that made my ears cry out.

"Ummm... Is Liam here?" I asked, gesturing inside the apartment.

"Na, this is Blue's spot. I think you got the wrong one?"

"Oh, this isn't H8?"

"That's around the corner. This is J8," she said, pointing to the faded door numbers.

"Oh, I'm sorry, I couldn't tell in the dark. I didn't mean to bother you," I apologized, pivoting on my feet and heading back towards my truck.

When I made it half way down the sidewalk, his voice came slicing through the air.

"Aye, why didn't you tell me someone was at the door?" he questioned the girl with a slight hint of irritation in his voice.

"Oh. She had the wrong apartment number," she explained.

Keeping up my pace, I made my way through the darkness before he could spot me and jumped back in my truck headed home.

If he could replace me so quick, then I guess he didn't give a fuck about me after all. Fuck Orion Alvarez! He could jump off the San Francisco Bridge for all I care. I had bigger things to worry about and from this point they didn't include him. I could solve my problems by myself. I guess it was me against the world.

Chapter 26: Blue

I had been blowing Kylani's phone up since last night. I knew it was her that came over to my apartment after I told the bust down to describe her to me. She probably thought I was dating ol' girl, but she was just someone I had let over to rock my mic. Between keeping tabs on my dad, making sure La was out of harm's way and keeping the streets in line, a nigga was stressed out.

Kylani knew how I felt about being ignored, so she was purposely sending me to voicemail to piss me off. Piranha was supposed to be tailing her today, so I called him. Picking up on the second ring, I heard a woman's voice before he said anything.

"Hello?"

"Aye, where you at?" I questioned.

"Over at the IHOP on Hatch. What's up?"

"I was calling to see if you had seen La today? I've been trying to call her, but she keeps forwarding me to voicemail."

"Uh, yea. That's the reason I'm out here on Hatch. She's out having breakfast with some nig..." he stopped himself when he realized he had said too much.

"She doing what?"

"Eating."

"I'll be there in twenty," I told him, hanging up the phone.

I wasn't one for that tit-for-tat bullshit. If I fuck up, then you tell me how you feel so we can fix it. Just because I let a bitch suck me off didn't mean she had to be in another nigga's face less than 24-hours later. La was about to feel me and she would wish she hadn't.

It took me all of 15 minutes to make it over to where P said they were. I didn't even bother to park my shit. I left it running by the door because I wasn't going to be in there long.

Piranha must have spotted me because he came running across the parking lot trying to stop me before I went inside, but he was too late. Scanning the restaurant, it took me less than five seconds to zero in on Kylani's face just as that nigga was about to brush the hair from in front of her eyes. I'm a jealous nigga, I can own that shit, and I'm very possessive. Don't touch what's mine unless you want to be missing some fingers, or your hand altogether. Together or not, La would always be mine so he was in violation.

"Blue…" Piranha started to say from behind me as I made my way over to the table.

By the time La's eyes met mine, it was too late because I was standing directly in front of her.

"My fault, Kylani. I tried to warn you he was coming," Piranha told her when he made his way over there, causing me to give him the side eye. I'd check him on it later, but for now I was focused on La and whoever this light skin nigga was.

"La, I'm only gonna say it once. Let's go," I growled through clenched teeth, keeping my eyes on ol' boy.

"Hey, man. What's up? I'm Chris."

"I wouldn't give a fuck if you were Obama himself. I ain't talking to you so don't talk to me," I snapped, looking down at his outreached hand like it was covered in shit.

"Blue. What are you doing here? You have no right to…"

"Wrong answer," I told her, looking her way for the first time as I pulled her from the booth.

"Aye!" Ol' boy started to say, pulling on my shirt. *Wrong move.* Hitting him with a right hook, I sent him flying backwards.

"Orion!" she yelled, finally standing up.

Throwing her over my shoulder, I made my way out of there before these white folks called the police and got me locked up. She was punching my back and cussing me out the whole time, but I paid her little ass no mind. I don't know why she felt the need to test me when I put her down and told her to get in the car, but the look in my eyes must have made her think twice because she got in the car pouting and slammed the door.

"Follow me," I instructed Piranha, making my way to the driver's side. Burning rubber all the way out the parking lot, I got this eerie feeling. Checking my rear-view mirror, the only car trailing me was Piranha's.

"How dare you? We're not together Ori…"

"Not now, La," I said, still checking my mirrors.

"What do you mean not now? That was bullshit! We not…"

"I SAID NOT NOW, LA!" I snapped, looking over in her direction. I felt bad for snapping on her, but sometimes I needed her to just listen when I asked her to do something. Taking the feeling as paranoia, I turned my attention back to the road and headed toward my spot.

Driving in silence for five minutes, I lowered the volume on the radio to apologize to La, but before I could speak the words shots rang out, hitting my car.

RAT TAT RAT TAT TAT TAT!

"GET DOWN!" I yelled.

Swerving in and out of traffic, I tried to make it to the nearest exit without either of us getting hit or wrecking my shit.

"You got a gun in here?" she asked just as the back window was shot out.

"Under my seat."

Reaching between my legs, she grabbed the gun and crawled in the backseat, keeping her head down as much as she could. The gun fire stopped for a split second and I swear she turned into one of them bitches from Charlie's Angels. Sending bullets through the windshield, I know for a fact that she hit someone because the car spun out of control and ran into a pole giving me just enough time to get off on the ramp.

Getting the fuck out of dodge, I changed routes and hit 80 mph all the way to my stash house taking every back road I could remember. Hitting Zane with a text, I let him know I was on my way with Piranha behind me. The only people that were gunning for me were Kylani's family and my dad. I wouldn't put shit past either one of them at this point.

I hit the block twice just to make sure I wasn't followed and when I saw I wasn't, I backed my car into the attached garage. Hitting the locks, I got out the car without speaking so much as two words to Kylani. I hadn't forgotten about the shit at IHOP, but I had to push that shit to the back of my mind for the time being.

"What the hell happened to y'all?" Zane questioned as he gave us the once over.

"Someone shot up my car leaving Hatch headed here," I explained.

"Where's Piranha?"

"Here I am." He walked in holding his arm, trying to stop the bleeding.

Kylani jumped up to help him. Telling Bullet what she needed, she tore a piece of his shirt off to access the damage. I sat back in awe as I watched her. For the first time I realized I didn't know this girl at all. The Kylani before me wasn't the same one I fell in love with. This one here was something from those Mob books. She was a trained shooter and could clean a wound better than most doctors. Not once during that whole shoot out did she panic, scream or lose her cool. She was just as calm as could be. Allowing her to finish up what she was doing, me, Zane and Bullet went into the other room.

"Did you get a look at who was shooting?" Bullet asked.

"Nah, man. All I know is that they were driving a black four-door Accord. I had a feeling some shit was about to pop off though. I had just snatched La out of IHOP from talking to some young nigga and we were driving for a few minutes before someone shot my shit up."

"Hol' up. La was out with a nigga?" Zane asked.

"Yea. Some lil' light bright nigga. Couldn't be no more than 19 or 20."

"Damn you must have fucked up bad. She done replaced yo' ass already," Zane laughed at the mug on my face. I swear this nigga wanted me to shoot him in the face.

"Like Beyonce' said in that one song nigga, *I'm Irreplaceable.*"

This clown only laughed harder, but what he failed to understand was that I was dead ass serious. Wasn't no getting rid of me. We were in this shit forever!

Chapter 27: Kylani

Orion storming into IHOP was the last thing I expected when I agreed to go on that date with Chris. Chris had given me his number a few weeks back after my break-up with Orion, but I never used his number until today. I only called him so he could keep my mind off the chick I saw leaving Orion's apartment last night, but that was wishful thinking because he blew my phone up for three hours straight until he popped up.

The shootout incident didn't help matters either. I could tell by the way he was staring at me that he looked at me differently now. The judgment was all in his eyes. It was one thing to hear something about someone, but it's another to witness it first-hand. If I didn't remain calm during everything, we could have both lost our lives and I wasn't done living yet so that was out of the question.

Finishing up my patch job on Piranha's arm, I smiled at him because I knew I was about to hear it from Orion.

"You think he's mad at me?" I whispered to him.

"Oh yea," he chuckled. "But I wouldn't sweat it too much. He may be mad, but he loves you," he added, trying to reassure me.

"He can't love me when he doesn't know the real me."

"And who's the real you?"

"A very misguided and broken girl. Like he told me before, I'm nothing more than a liar and a thief and I'm pretty sure now I'm a murderer," I vented, pushing my hair out of my face.

155

"You ain't broken. On the real, you a survivor. We've talked over the past few weeks and that person was the real you. What you do is nothing more than the way you were raised. If you were taught to be a certain way, then no one can blame you for who you turn out to be. It's all about how you handle the situation."

"Thanks, Piranha," I smiled weakly at him. "I've been meaning to ask you since the moment you introduced yourself. What's your real name?"

"Pernell."

"Well, why do they call you Piranha?"

"You'd rather not know." He gave me this smirk that I couldn't quite read, but taking his word for it I dropped the conversation.

"P, can I talk to La alone please?" I heard Orion say from behind me.

Tapping me lightly on the shoulder, he got up and walked out the room to where I'm guessing the rest of the guys were.

"How did we get here, ma?"

"Lying," was the only answer that seemed right.

"Who was that nigga from earlier?"

"You don't get to do that."

"Do what?"

"To act like you give a fuck!" I snapped, turning in his direction.

"You honestly think that I go around making a habit of pulling chicks out of restaurants? Be real, baby girl. You and I both know that I ain't that type of nigga," he answered, waving me off.

"You walked away from me! Then when I finally had enough of this stupid ass fight, I swallowed my pride and came to make things right with you only to be met by a bitch at your door, so if I want to spend time with the next nigga then I will!"

"Yea, if you and that nigga want me to speak at y'all funeral then by all means, do you ma."

"I don't even know why I try," I mumbled, shaking my head. Getting up from where I was sitting, I tried to walk away when he grabbed my arm and turned me around to face him.

"You try because you love me just as I love you. You try because you tired of fighting and you ready for us to get back on track. Look, I fucked up when I walked away from you that day and for that I'm sorry. And I didn't fuck the chick you saw coming out of my apartment last night. I could have, but I didn't. Now I ain't apologizing about the shit that happened today. You can't blame a man for going crazy when he sees the woman he loves all in the next nigga's face. You better be glad that all I did was punch his ass," he told me, keeping me in place with his hands on my waist.

Rolling my eyes at him, I could do nothing but laugh at his attempt of an apology. Hearing him say that he loved me had my heart doing laps around my chest and I wanted nothing more than for us to get past the bullshit.

"This is the only chance you get. We both fucked up and for that I'm willing to try this over again, but just know that I match your crazy. I better not see ol' girl back around again," I warned him.

"Oh, so you a gangsta now, huh?" he smirked.

"You know what they say. You gotta watch out for them quiet ones," I joked.

"Yea, yea," he laughed, pulling me closer into his chest.

"And Orion?"

"What's up?"

"I love you too."

"I know, baby girl," he replied, kissing me in the top on the head.

"Man, it's about time y'all asses made up. I was about two seconds away from shooting this nigga in the foot if he caught one more attitude with me," Zane said, stepping into the doorway. Leave it up to him to say some crazy shit.

"Fuck you, nigga," Orion joked, flicking him off.

Watching as they went back and forth with snide remarks, I felt at peace for the first time in weeks and I knew that with Orion in my corner I didn't need anything or anyone else. I knew that this was just the peace and quiet before the storm, but nothing could prepare me for what came my way next.

Chapter 28: Zane

The shootout that Blue and La had that day was just the first of many. Traps got burned down, two of our corner boys got knocked and police started snooping around. Police had never been an issue for as long as me and Blue been in business together, but the moment we fall out with his bitch ass daddy, they appear out of thin air.

This shit had Blanco's name written all over it, and even though Blue never said it out loud, I knew he was conflicted about the shit he found out from his mom. He was going to bat with the only parent he had over the only woman he ever loved other than his aunt and the reason was still unclear.

No matter how many people told us the story, the only common factor was that this beef started with Blanco and Leilani, but everything else was a jumbled mess. The only person who could shed light on what was going on was the motherfucker gunning for us.

The shit was a constant headache, and I was regretting our decision to come to Cali in the first place, but I was down to ride for my nigga any and every day of the week so it was only right we went through the motions together.

Word got back to our new connect, Rock, about the drama we had going on and he gave us two weeks to find a solution to our problems or he was taking his business elsewhere. Now I fear no nigga alive breathing, but I had a level of respect for Rock. He was in his late twenties and moved more work than a little bit. I researched everyone we came in contact with, so it wasn't hard to hear about how he had the game sewed up.

Checking on one of the leads that Bullet gave me, I sat outside the house of some older lady. From what I could tell, she was in her early 60's. Bullet said that she was connected to Blanco in more ways than one and since this nigga had officially become a ghost, I was following every lead I could to track him down.

Receiving a text message on my phone, I started to ignore it, but something told me to stop what I was doing and look at it.

Blue: Meet me over at Memorial

Who the hell could be at Memorial? Putting down my phone, I started my car and headed toward the hospital to see what was going on, but what I didn't know was that someone had spotted me.

* * * *

Following Blue's instructions, I made my way up to the third floor where the Intensive Care Unit was. Fearing the worst, I jogged all the way down the hallway to the family room once I got off the elevator.

Walking in the waiting room, the first face I saw was the dude that Kylani introduced us to at her graduation, Rylan. It was something off about the nigga, but I couldn't put my finger on it. Like, that nigga's whole aura was just off. I wasn't sure what it was, but if he kept eyeing me the way he was I would show him why the fuck I was fifty shades past crazy.

Swaggering my way over to where I saw the crew sitting at, I sat down closest to Blue but kept my eyes locked on La's family. The only one that seemed genuinely hurt was La, so it definitely had me wondering why the hell I was here.

"What's going on?"

"They found La's dad in his office not breathing earlier today. They just called her because they don't know if he gone' make it," Blue explained, looking in the same direction I was staring in.

"How long y'all been up here?"

"Bout thirty minutes at the most. But let me holla at you out in the hallway right quick."

Following his lead, I trailed behind him as he walked away from the waiting room down the hallway towards the vending machines.

"Something ain't adding up."

"What you mean?" I asked.

"Did you notice how no one else in there seemed broken up about this shit besides La?"

Catching what he was saying, I simply nodded my head and waited for him to finish.

"I need to talk to La and see if she suspects anything, but if shit go left I need you to handle that for me."

"Say less," I nodded, letting him know I would handle it.

"But how did that lead pan out?" he asked, glancing down toward the waiting room.

"No one was there from what I saw. I sat on the spot for three hours and no one came or left and it's in a cul-de-sac so I would have seen them if they did."

"Alright. Whenever we find out what's going on with baby girl's dad, I'll ride back over there with you."

"Bet."

A gut wrenching scream coming from the waiting room made me snap my head in that direction as I tried to keep up with Blue. I swear that nigga turned into a track star in a matter of seconds. Stepping into view, Kylani was on the floor rocking back and forth with tears streaming down her face so I already knew what that meant. The doctor was attempting to offer his condolences, but every word he spoke went through one ear and out the other.

Slipping out the room behind him, I stopped him to ask a few questions.

"Ayo, Doc."

"How can I help you?"

"I'm the nephew of the deceased and I showed up late. Do you mind telling me what happened?"

"As I was explaining to the wife and son earlier, he wasn't breathing when the paramedics brought him in, but we were able to jump start his heart again. However, the lack of oxygen caused his brain to hemorrhage and he fell into a coma. Performing emergency surgery, we stopped the bleeding on his brain, but he died on the table."

"Do you know what could have caused him to stop breathing?"

"There could have been several reasons. Heart attack, stroke, there could have been toxins or something affecting the lungs causing them to collapse, but we should know more when they perform the autopsy."

"Alright, thank you Doc. When you get the results in, you can call my cell if you can't get in touch with my aunt or my cousin. I'll be the one handling all the funeral arrangements."

"No problem, and again I'm sorry for your loss," he replied, turning to walk away.

Feeling like someone was watching me, I turned around and connected eyes with Rylan again. The nigga was watching my every move and I'm sure he would tell them he saw me talking to the doctor. Knowing this nigga would be a problem, I put my fingers in the shape of a gun and pointed it at that nigga and hit his ass with a smirk before swaggering out of the hospital. He didn't know his days were numbered. Fucking around with me that nigga was about to come up missing.

Chapter 29: Blue

It had been three days since baby girl's dad died and she was like a shell of her former self. Most of the time she wouldn't answer her phone and she hadn't been out of her condo since she went in it. Shit was getting more hectic out in the streets for me, so when I wasn't around the guys took turns keeping an eye on her for me.

I had given her as much time as I could, but I needed her to snap out of it. I know it sounds harsh, but that nigga wasn't coming back and I needed her to face that fact. Pulling out the spare key I made to her apartment, it looked like a tornado had run through this bitch full speed. There were Chinese food containers, dirty cups and a pizza box in the living room. Down the hallway was no better. There were clothes making a trail all the way to her room.

When I walked into her room, I was ready to walk out again. I loved lil mama to death, but she had this room sounding off. Flicking on the light switch, I couldn't see her ass buried underneath her covers. I walked into the adjoining bathroom in her room, turned on the water, got the temperature the way I wanted and walked back in the room to get her.

Seeing her feet playing peek-a-boo from the bottom of the bed, I grabbed her ankles and snatched her from the covers. Carrying her in the bathroom like she was a baby, I threw her ass in the tub, clothes on and all. Gasping for air like a fish out of water, I sat on the toilet lid and refused to let her get out of the shower until she snapped out of whatever it was she had going on.

"Blueeee... It's so coldddd." She got out as best she could as her teeth chattered.

"I know. I'll be back in an hour and I expect you to be out the shower, dressed and ready to go," I told her, swaggering out the bathroom and closing the door behind me.

"Oh yea, and make sure you clean up this nasty ass apartment too!" I yelled through the closed door. She was pissed, but she'd get over it. I couldn't be with someone that fell apart and came undone at the seams when tragedy struck. I need someone that was built Ford tough and even though I could see it in her, I needed La to see it in herself. It may not seem like it now, but she would be alright with time.

Driving over to IHOP, I ordered us both some breakfast to go before making my way back over to her spot. I wasn't surprised to see she had straightened up. I couldn't baby her forever. Sometimes tough love is just what the doctor ordered, and this was one of those times.

"How you feeling?" I asked her, bringing the food in and sitting it down on the table.

"Better. Thanks," she said just above a whisper.

"Come talk to me," I instructed her, tapping the spot on my lap.

Like the big kid she was, she sat on my lap and snuggled up to me as I ran my fingers through her hair. She took a few minutes to gather her thoughts, but when she did she cried softly. I wanted nothing more than to take her pain away, but this one was out of my control. Laying my head back on the sofa, I continued to rock her until she was ready to talk.

"I never got a chance to talk to him. I was supposed to go hang out with him today. We had planned a day out, just me and him. I was going to tell him everything. About me. About you. Your dad. I was going to tell it all. But...," her voice trailed off as she broke into sobs again.

"La? I need you to listen to me, alright?" Feeling the slight nod of her head, I kept talking.

"You stronger than this, ma. The constant thoughts of what could've been done and what should've been will drive you insane and you can't do that to yourself. Cry as much as you need to, feel sorry for your dad and his time being ended short, but after you cry I need you to leave it all here. I'll stay with you as long as I need to today, but after this we need to focus on our next move."

I wasn't sure when I fell asleep, but the hook to one of my favorite Kevin Gates song woke me up as it blared from my cell phone. Checking the time, I saw that we had slept the whole day away. It was almost ten o'clock at night. Looking at the caller ID, I saw Zane's name. Thinking it was important, I answered it before it could go to voicemail.

"Talk to me."

"Where the hell you at?"

"Last time I checked, I was grown and we ain't fucking so state your peace or get off my line."

"Pipe down with all that rah-rah shit. I was calling because yo' ass was supposed to meet me over three hours ago and you still ghost. Now again, where the fuck you at?"

"Damn, I forgot. I was over here with La."

"Say less. I can handle this. Tell baby sis she gone' be aight," he told me. Even though Zane wasn't feeling the whole idea of La in the beginning, he put his ill thoughts to the side and dealt with her off the strength of me and that's all that a nigga could ask for.

"I got you. But let me go, a nigga gotta piss like a motherfucka," I told him. We exchanged a few more words before I disconnected the call. Lifting La's legs off my lap, I tried to be as quiet as possible as I made my way to the bathroom. Handling my business, I washed my hands and headed back to the living room where she was sleeping on the couch.

Leaning against the door way leading into the living room, I stood there for a minute and just watched her. It seems like some creep shit, but if you've ever loved someone as much as I loved La, you'd stare at them for no reason at all and wonder what they think about and if it had something to do with you. Walking over to where she lay, I kneeled down in front of the couch and planted soft kisses on her exposed shoulder and the side of her face until she stirred out of her sleep.

Opening her eyes to look at me, she gave me a weak smile before sitting up and stretching.

"What time is it?" she asked, stifling a yawn.

"A quarter to eleven. How'd you sleep?"

"The best I have in the past few days."

"That's good. But go handle your business in the bathroom and then come back in here. There's something I need to talk to you about."

"Kay. Gimme a kiss." She puckered her lips and leaning over.

"No, ma'am. I need you to tackle that breath first. I love you ma, but I don't love you that much to be kissing you with your breath smelling like gym socks." I laughed at the look on her face. That shit was priceless.

"Fuck you! My breath does not stink!" she yelled, flicking me off with her other hand over her mouth.

"Then why are you covering up your mouth?" I joked.

Punching me in the arm, she stormed down the hall and slammed the door to the bathroom.

"Make sure you use mouth wash too!"

I could hear her cussing me out and all I could do was laugh. When she finished, she came back into the living room pouting. Instead of babying her like she wanted me to, I let her throw her little tantrum and sit on the couch opposite me.

"What did you want to talk about?"

"I wouldn't ask you this unless I really needed to know, so don't get all defensive when I do."

"Spit it out, Orion."

"Do you think your mom and your brother could have killed your pops?" I asked, staring at her to gauge her reaction.

"No! Why would you ask me something like that?" she snapped,-*-9 jumping to her feet.

"Calm down. I asked because Zane talked to the doctor at the night of the hospital and he said that your dad could have either had a stroke or heart attack."

"That's impossible. My dad was a health nut. He exercised five times a week, and he didn't even smoke. Hell, he barely ever drank anything."

"Which brings me to the other thing that the doctor said. From what I understand, he said that the only other possible cause was that a toxin infected his lungs and caused them to collapse."

"Toxin? Like poison?" she questioned incredulously.

"Yea, but we won't know anything until tomorrow. They performed his autopsy and now we're just waiting on the results."

"Oh my God. I know my mom hated my guts, but she loved my dad," she tried to explain and I think it was more so for her benefit than mine.

"I need you to take over your family's business."

"Orion, you know how I feel about that. I told you that I didn't…"

"I know La, I know. But listen to me, your dad wanted you to take over for a reason. He had to have known something was up or else he would have given it to your brother as planned. If somebody is working with my dad, it has to either be your brother and your mother and you said so yourself that your mom hates your guts and your brother doesn't think for himself. If they take over your family business and they link up with my dad, they will become the most powerful organization that ever ran the West Coast and could expand out East and my dad has connections overseas. That's why you and I will take over both. If I can take down my dad, that makes me the next head of the Trinidad cartel, and if you take over like you're supposed to, you become the next mafia princess." I explained everything as best I could.

I needed Kylani to see the bigger picture. At this point it was kill or be killed, and I knew that first chance they got that they would kill us without question. Family or no family.

"I don't know."

"I'm going to keep it a buck with you since we practicing this whole honesty thing. Me and you are no more than liabilities. We know too much and if we not going with the flow of things, then we going against the grain. There is nothing stopping them from taking us out and let's be clear, there are five of us altogether. Me, you, Zane, Bullet, and Piranha. We got a team full of soldiers, but they owe me nothing because I haven't known them that long and they can be sold to the highest bidder. As much as I want to say that we them niggas on the streets, that's not enough to withstand an army of motherfuckers. You can think about it, but I need you to think about surviving because your decision will either make or break the team. With or without you, I'm killing Blanco. No questions asked. The question is, can you do the same?"

The shit was a lot to process, so I wouldn't pressure her into answering right away, but I needed Kylani to understand that it was more than she thought it was. Laying everything out on the table, I hoped she makes the right decision and fast. We had too much at stake and failing was not an option.

Chapter 30: Kylani

Trying to process everything that Orion said, he had a point but I couldn't make myself believe that my family had anything to do with my dad's death. If they really did, then I couldn't live with myself. I had a chance to tell him about the supposed beef that Blanco had with him and the possibility of someone working with him to get rid of me, but I didn't, and as much as I told myself that it was because I didn't have enough proof, I knew that wasn't true. I didn't tell him because I knew if I spoke the words out loud to anyone other than myself, it would make them true.

Pushing the thoughts into the back of my mind, I headed to meet up with Orion's mom at the mall. I had found her number in his phone and asked her to meet up with me. She seemed to know more about my family than I did so it was only right I asked her to help me understand.

Slipping my body into a teal floral dress, I pulled my hair into a tight bun on the top of my head and set the outfit off with some all-white low cut Chuck Taylor's. I could only be so girly, and knowing we were going into the mall to shop, I would not be walking around in wedges or sandals. My feet would hate me.

Giving myself the once over in the mirror, I applied a light coat of lip gloss to my lip and inspected the cut on my forehead. The cut had finally healed and the stitches had dissolved. My shoulder was still sore and it would take a minute before I could function back at a hundred percent, but I was moving around as if nothing ever happened. Placing my Gucci shades on top of my head, I grabbed my keys and was ready to go.

* * * *

Walking into the food court at the mall, I texted his mom and told her where I was. I grabbed a milk shake and sat down and enjoyed it as I waited for her to join me.

"Kylani, is that you?" I heard someone ask from above me.

Bringing my eyes up, they were met by Chris' friendly face. I felt bad about our botched date at IHOP, but I was glad to see he was doing okay.

"Hey, Chris. How are you?" I stood up and gave him a quick hug.

Feeling him wince when I touched him, I looked at him with concern. He could never be my man, but I still considered him somewhat of a friend.

"Are you okay?"

"Yea. Summer training for football started Monday and I'm still a little sore from the practice. I got banged up pretty good," he chuckled.

"Oh, okay. How's that going?" I asked, sitting back down in my seat.

"It's fun. Can't believe I'm actually playing college football though. I wanted to go semi-pro, but that wasn't in my future. Do you mind?" he asked, gesturing towards the empty seat across from me.

"No, go ahead," I replied, giving him the okay. Ms. Linda had just texted and said that she was fifteen minutes away so I could use the company until she got here.

Spending time with Chris was cool. He helped me forget about all my problems and reminded me that I was a teenager. I was always so worried about trying to make my mom love me and making my dad proud of me that I never got to do the normal things. Sharing chili cheese fries, we joked around and talked about everything under the sun. I could be someone completely different with Chris and not worry about him judging me. I didn't have to be a Vendetti. I could just be Kylani.

"Kylani sweetheart, I'm sorry I'm late. I forgot my purse and had to turn all the way back around and go get it. Who's your friend?" she questioned, eyeing Chris.

"Oh, this is Chris. Chris, this is Ms. Linda, Orion's mom," I said, making the introductions.

"Nice to meet you, ma'am. La, it was nice running into you. I should be getting out of here. Hopefully, I'll see you around soon," he smiled, standing up from the table.

"It was nice seeing you too." I smiled and waved as he walked away.

Ms. Linda was watching him like a hawk as he swaggered towards the exit. Keeping her eyes on him until he was completely gone, she finally turned around and gave me her attention.

"I don't like him."

"Who, Chris? He's harmless enough," I replied, waving her off.

"I know you barely know me and what I think doesn't really matter to you, but watch out for him, okay?"

Hearing the concern in her voice, I knew that she was just looking out for me. Agreeing to be careful, we made a day out of shopping. My mind kept wondering back to Chris. I told Ms. Linda that I would keep an eye on him, but he was my friend. No more, no less. I wasn't dumb enough to tell Orion that I ran in to him, but I was interested in keeping Chris around as a friend. Something told me I would regret that decision, but for now I would go with the flow.

Chapter 31: Amari

What was supposed to be a one or two-time thing, turned into something I did at least twice a day. I was snorting more cocaine than I liked to admit, but the feeling kept me on cloud nine. The day my dad died, I started consuming more and more. I know that I was helping plot to betray him, but that didn't mean I wanted to see him dead. When I was sober my conscious ate away at me, so I stayed as high as I could so I could forget what I had done.

My mom keeps telling me that everything was for our benefit and to not worry about anything. Ever since my dad died, she's been sneaking around on the phone and Rylan had been questioning me more and more on whether I was ready to put the plan into motion to get rid of Kylani.

It's like the nigga went from being in love with her to being obsessed with her and everything she's been doing since she no longer lives with us. The nigga was on some fatal attraction shit and in a way I wanted to warn La, but that would basically be putting a target on my own back.

Finally finding what I came in the basement for, I slowly ascended the stairs until I heard my mom's voice in the kitchen. Stopping to listen, I pressed my ear to the door and tried to make out what she was saying.

"We have to wait until after the funeral when all the money clears before I transfer anything…. The deal was for 3 million not a penny more… you didn't even take care of the little bitch so don't give me that bullshit! Take care of it and I'll add the rest that you're asking for... don't call this phone again unless it's done!"

There were a few seconds of silence before I heard something crash into the wall. Sitting down on the steps, I wrecked my brain trying to figure out who she was talking to on the phone. Knowing she was talking about La, I battled with the decision to warn her. On one hand, she was my sister and I loved her, but I knew that if she was dead I would be next in line and I would have her part of our dad's inheritance. It didn't take long for me to take the latter. Hell, better her than me.

Chapter 32: Anonymous

I wasn't ready to let my presence be known to those around me, but when I did I knew the revelation would shake shit up. I had been watching Kylani for a while now. Something about her intrigued me in every way. I heard the whispers about the Vendetti family. To most people it meant little. They seemed like just another rich family, but to the underground their name alone spoke volumes.

I was just about ready to make my move on her when that out of town nigga appeared out of thin air. I wasn't tripping at first because it didn't look serious, but not too long afterwards he started running with her at the park, going on dates, playing basketball together and keeping time. I was sure the night they had that fight in the parking lot of Steak N Shake that was the end of this little fling, but he showed back up and they were back on track.

It was time to put my plans into motion. I was tired of playing about what's mine. She doesn't know it yet, but Kylani is my future wife and if she denied me then I had no problem making sure no one else would have her either. Pulling out my cell phone, I laid my head back on the headrest and closed my eyes as I waited for the person to answer.

"Hello?"

"I need a favor."

"You need me to send a message or just a warning?"

"Both. Make sure somebody gets hit, but not fatal. I need them to feel me."

"Done," was all the person said before the line went dead.

The thought alone made my dick hard. Sending the information and pictures through a text message, I looked up at Kylani's bedroom window once more before starting my car and heading home. In due time, Kylani and her little boy toy would feel my presence and I couldn't wait!

Chapter 33: Zane

Riding through the city, me and Blue were doing our weekly pick-ups. Since the traps had been getting hit and we had the cops snooping around, we felt it would be best to handle the pickups and drop offs. These lil' niggas didn't owe us nothing more than what they were giving us. We hadn't done enough or proved ourselves enough to earn that die hard loyalty, so it was better safe than sorry.

I've been getting this nagging feeling on and off for the past few days since Kylani's dad died. I wasn't sure what it was, but it was getting stronger. I knew something was about to happen, but I didn't know when or what it was. The shit was like being stalked by a ghost in those horror movies. You know the threat is there, but you can't see it.

Pulling up to our trap over on Vermont, I saw one of our runners named Zak. He couldn't have been no older than nineteen, but he had the heart of a lion so I didn't knock his hustle. Giving the niggas on the outside of the house a head nod, we made our way in the house and saw they had everything running smoothly. This house sold nothing but pills. Mollies, handle bars, blue dolphins, percs, oxies and anything else that came into a pill form was sold out of this house.

"Where Python at?" Blue asked one of the bitches that were bagging in the kitchen.

"In the basement."

Down in the basement, we spotted him over at a table running the money through the money counter before rubber banding it and throwing it in a duffle.

"What's the word?" I asked, walking over to the table dapping him up.

"Not shit. I thought y'all said y'all would be here in two hours?" he asked, ashing his blunt.

"Change of plans," was all Blue said to him before he checked the bags.

"How much is this?"

"A little over 30 bands. We gotta re-up tonight or in the morning. What the girls bagging up is the last of what we got," he explained, finishing up his count.

"I'll come back by tomorrow morning with something for you," I told him.

"Alright, bet," he responded, sticking the last couple stacks in the counter, banded em' up and stuck it with the rest of the stacks in the bag.

"Dat's all of it. I'll stick whatever we make tonight in the safe for next week's pick-up."

"Bet," we said in unison before grabbing a duffle bag a piece and heading back to the main floor of the house.

That eerie feeling washed over me again as I felt the small of my back for my guns. The look on my face must have alerted Blue because he stopped walking and grabbed his heat.

"You aight, my nigga?"

"Ion know, but we 'bout to find out," I told him as we headed towards the front door.

Right as I put my handle on the knob, shots broke out, shattering the windows and sending these bitches into a frenzy. I will never understand why when some shit popped off, a female's first instinct is to scream like that shit would do something.

Hitting the ground, I pulled out my twin nines before standing back up and snatching the door open, returning fire. Most people would have called it reckless, but I wasn't about to duck and dodge. If it was my time to go then so be it, but I'd go out letting my gun clap back.

Hearing gunshots from behind me, I didn't have to look back to know that it was Blue. Letting them thangs bark, I shot at the car until it was out of sight. Checking around at the damage, I saw at least three of the lil niggas that were outside were hit somewhere, but the shots weren't fatal.

"Zane!" I heard Blue call from behind me.

I saw him standing in the door way of the house waving me over. Double checking my surroundings, I had to make sure these niggas were dumb enough to double back around. When I saw the coast was clear, I made my way back in the house.

One of the girls that was bagging up was laid out on the floor with a bullet in the neck and the other was hit in the leg, but other than that she was fine. The chick that wasn't hit, was sitting in the corner crying loud as hell and she was pissing me off.

Pointing one of my guns in her direction, I cocked the hammer before letting one off just inches away from her head.

"Shut all that fucking screaming or the next one gone' be in your dome," I snapped, looking at her.

Covering her mouth with her hand, she nodded her head vigorously trying not to piss on herself. I was actually surprised that I still had a bullet left because I was just trying to scare her, but I got my point across either way so I wasn't tripping.

"Even though we in the hood, them boys gone' be here in a minute. Yo, put this shit in the trunk and make this shit quick!" Blue barked out orders.

Taking the other duffle bags to the car, I grabbed the bottle of Henny I had underneath my seat and a towel I used to wash my car.

"Aye, you got a lighter?" I asked Blue when he came outside.

"Here," he said tossing it to me. Stuffing the tip of the towel in to the bottle as much as I could, I lit the end of the towel and walked inside the house.

"I suggest if you in here that you leave if you want to live," I warned, throwing the bottle against the curtains in the kitchen and walking back out like I didn't do nothing.

Light jogging back to my car, I jumped in and burnt rubber all the way down the street. If those niggas was still there when the cops showed up that was on them. I had never been to jail and I wasn't about to go today. Shit was getting real out here, and it was only a matter of time before a full-blown war started up. Always down to ride for mines, I would make a motherfucker regret the day they looked at me twice, let alone shot at me. Allow me to reintroduce myself, I'm "that nigga."

Chapter 34: Blue

I swear, niggas was bold when they were on that Casper bullshit. I had been searching high and low trying to find Blanco's bitch ass and that nigga was hiding better than a snake in a tree. I couldn't believe I had been shot at not once, but twice in the past few weeks. I never had a nigga test me back home, so the shit was foreign to me now that a motherfucker was doing it.

Blanco knew how I gave it up, so when I caught up with his ass he was in for a real treat. He thought he taught me everything I knew, but you never let your right hand know what the left is doing. I wouldn't be a man if I had to hold his hand. He may have given me my start in the game, but I'm the one that made all this shit possible.

I was about to show him the side of me I showed these niggas in the streets. My name didn't have niggas shook for no reason. Trying to keep my anger under control, I paced around my warehouse trying to figure out how the fuck them niggas knew where I would be.

Picking up my ringing cell phone, I saw the number was blocked. Pressing the ignore button, I sat it back down and started pacing again. Not even ten seconds later, it rang again.

"WHAT?!" I roared, answering on the third ring.

"Is that any way to speak to yo father?"

"Nigga, fuck you! You ain't shit to me, believe that!"

This nigga had nuts the size of gorillas for calling me. Today must be test Blue day or something. The sound of his voice only added fuel to my flame.

"Tsk- tsk, Blue. I hear you looking for me now. What can I do for you?" he laughed in my ear.

"If you wasn't hiding like the pussy you is then you would know why. When you aimed at me, you should have made sure you killed me. When I find you, I'm gone' forget that I came out yo' wrinkled ass nut sack!" I spat, hanging up. No other words needed to be spoken. He wanted a problem with me and now he had one.

Dialing another number on my phone, I waited until the person answered before I told them what I needed. I needed to disappear for a while for the shit that I had planned.

* * * *

Waking up the next morning to someone banging on my door like they had lost they damn mind had me pissed off. Checking the clock, it was only eight in the morning and I had just got in at six. Sliding on some basketball shorts, I grabbed my gun from my bedside table before answering it.

Snatching it open, I aimed my gun and immediately regretted not asking who it was. *Fuck!*

"Orion Jay Alvarez?" the officer asked, putting his hand on his gun.

"Who's asking?" I asked, lowering my gun. I had seen too many stories on the news about them shooting unarmed black men and I knew they would gladly pop my ass and say they felt threatened.

"We have a warrant for your arrest. Please drop the gun and step outside," he instructed.

Disassembling my gun, I sat it on the floor beside me.

"Show me the warrant and I will," I told him.

Flashing it in my face, he snatched me out the door and threw me on the ground just as Kylani came into view.

"Oh my God! Blue, what's going on?"

"Go in the house and call Zane. Tell him to call my lawyer and to meet me at the police station," I commanded. Tears formed in her eyes and my heart broke.

"Kylani, focus! Do what I said. Go call Zane. Now!" I was being hard on her, but her tears wouldn't help me at all.

She disappeared inside my apartment as the police escorted me to the police car. As he read me my rights, the only word that stuck out was murder. This was some bullshit. Ducking my head to get in the squad car, I locked eyes with Kylani. Mouthing that I loved her, I turned my head once I saw the tears fall. Out of all the shit I could get locked up for, it was this. A nigga couldn't win for losing. Fuck my life!

Chapter 35: Kylani

My life had been similar to a domino effect over the past few months. If it wasn't one thing, then it was another. I was waiting on Zane and Orion's lawyer to meet me at the police station. One of the officers that arrested Orion tried to stay around and search his place, but I wouldn't let him in without a warrant. I'm glad I pulled up when I did.

I had come over to check on him. He had called me yesterday to check on me because of the shootout they had at one of his traps. He was convinced that his dad had something to do with it, but I wasn't so sure. I felt that a man of his status wouldn't need to use shooters to get a point across. There was more to the story than what we were seeing. One of my biggest regrets is not telling my dad about everything that was going on. He would be able to fill in the blanks, but with him gone I was left to find the answers myself. Only problem is that I don't know where to look.

Footsteps approaching me caused me to raise my head. I breathed a sigh of relief when I saw that it was Zane and a tall white man that I assumed was Orion's lawyer. Standing up to greet them, I broke down in Zane's arm.

"Straighten up, ma. You know that Blue wouldn't want you falling to pieces."

"I guess you're right," I told him, straightening up.

"You know I'm right. La, this is the best Jew in the game, Baiyler. Baiyler, this is Orion's girl, Kylani."

"I see what Mr. Alvarez sees in you. I promise I will take good care of him." He shook my hand before walking in the back.

"So what do we do now?" I asked Zane.

"We wait and see what happens. I'ma be real with you, sis. They got him on a Friday afternoon, so unless Baiyler can work out some kind of magic and get him a bail hearing before five, he's most likely gone spend the weekend locked up."

"But my dad's funeral is Sunday."

"And as fucked up as it may be, he may miss it."

I would be lying if I said that my heart wasn't hurting. I don't know if I could forgive him if he missed my dad's funeral. He didn't ask to be locked up, but he was the cause of it. It sounds selfish, but it was how I felt. I need him to be there for me and knowing that may be impossible, angered me.

His lawyer was in the back for almost an hour before he came back out. The sober look on his face let me know he didn't have good news. Preparing myself for the worse, I walked over to him cautiously.

"Well, I have good news and bad news. Orion was arrested for second degree murder and they want to keep him, but the good news is they don't have any evidence so it's circumstantial. It may take a few hours, but since they do not have any real evidence then they have to let him go," he explained.

"Thank God."

"Did they say who the person was?" Zane asked.

"A twenty-year old by the name of Bishop Grace."

Seeing Zane's jaw flex from my peripheral, I knew this had to be someone they knew. When the lawyer went to make sure they were processing Orion's release, I followed behind Zane as he stormed outside.

"What's wrong? Who is this Bishop person?"

"I'll let Blue tell you. It's not my place," he told me.

I wasn't a saint, but a murder charge? Shit was spiraling out of control and I was just ready for it to end.

* * * *

The ride back to my apartment was a quiet one. I hadn't said more than ten words to Orion since he got out. I was exhausted, and all I wanted to do was take a shower and get in the bed.

"So you givin' me the silent treatment or what's up?" he asked, breaking the silence when I pulled into the parking lot to my place.

"I'm just tired. I've had a very eventful day," I replied, getting out as I got out the truck.

"Bullshit. What's your problem?"

"I said nothing, Orion."

"Fuck it then." He pushed past me as we made our way inside my apartment.

I wasn't about to feed into his temper tantrum. I went to my room and gathered my clothes for my shower. When I found what I wanted to wear, I placed my phone on the charger and headed to the bathroom. Lathering the scrubber up with my Dove body wash, I tried my best to scrub my stress away. I wasn't even in the shower a good five minutes before the door swung open causing the air to move the shower current.

"Are you fucking this nigga?" Orion yelled, grabbing me by my arm almost causing me to bust my ass in the shower.

"Fucking who?"

"Don't play dumb with me! Are you fucking that little nigga from IHOP?"

"Why would you even ask me some bullshit like that? If you want to hear me say it then fine. No, I'm not fucking him, Orion."

"Then why the fuck is this nigga texting your phone asking when can he see you again?!" he yelled, throwing my phone against the wall causing it to shatter.

Fuck! I could kick myself for leaving my phone in there, but I had nothing to hide so I thought nothing of it. When I said nothing to defend myself, he just shook his head.

"Man, fuck this shit. You won't have me looking like a fucking dummy for yo' ass. If you want that nigga tell him he can have you," he told me and stormed out the bathroom.

"Orion, wait! It's not like that. Let me explain!" I pleaded, jumping out the shower trying to keep him from leaving.

192

"Explain what? If you feel like explaining, then tell my why this nigga got your number, huh?"

"Because I gave it to him," I told him, putting my head down.

"Damn. I never pegged you as a hoe," he spat, turning around to walk away again.

"Nigga, you wish! I ain't never been a hoe and never will be."

"Just a liar, huh?" he threw over his shoulder.

"I'm the only liar, though? I haven't lied to you since we got back together. I've told you everything, and this is what I have to deal with? I sat in a cold ass police station for five fucking hours waiting for you to be released on a murder charge. Murder, Orion?"

"I DIDN'T FUCKING ASK YOU TO! You want a fucking medal because you did what the fuck you were supposed to do? You're my woman. If something ever happens to me or I find myself in a jam, you're supposed to be there at the drop of a fucking dime because that's what real woman do. They ride. And don't throw me being locked up for murder in my face because you a fucking saint, right? You don't rob motherfuckas for a living, huh?"

"Fuck you!" I screamed, turning my back to him walk back into my room.

"This the shit we not gone' do," he said, turning me around and backing me into the wall.

"I'm not a fucking mind reader, Kylani. If there is something I'm not doing then you gotta say something. You should never run to another nigga, especially about what the fuck I got going on. But what's bothering me is that you feel so comfortable speaking on me to the next nigga, so I will ask you again. Are you fucking him, Kylani?" he asked, looking me in the eyes.

"No," I told him, staring him in the eyes.

He stared at me for a few minutes searching my eyes before he pulled me into him.

"My fault. I shouldn't have called you a hoe, but whatever the fuck you got going on with that nigga, you need to dead that shit immediately. On everything I love, Kylani, if I see his name or number in your phone again, I will not hesitate to slap the dog shit out of you before I kill his ass and make you watch. Do you understand me?" he said, speaking directly into my ear.

The feel of his body pressed against my bare skin caused me to hesitate before I finally answered him.

"Y…yes."

Looking in my eyes, he must've seen the lust behind them because he ran his hand from my thigh, up my chest until he was applying light pressure to my neck.

"Are you sure?" he questioned in a husky voice, squeezing lightly.

"Yes. Now move," I replied, trying to push him off of me. Even though I was horny, I was not feeling him at all right now.

"Uh-huh. I don't know if you know it or not, but you mine til death do us part. I tatted my name on this pussy the first time you let me in it so that makes it mine."

"Don't kid yourself. Don't nothing over here belong to you as long as it's attached to my body. Now like I said before, move!" I said, shoving him off of me.

I put a light switch in my step as I walked my naked ass back in my room. Being lifted off my feet caused me to scream out before I went flying on my bed face first.

"Move, and I will make it worse," he warned. I could hear him taking off his clothes behind me, but I was too scared to move.

"Up on all fours," he demanded, smacking me on my ass as he got on the bed behind me.

Assuming the position, I got on all fours. Feeling him place himself at my entrance, I braced myself for the ride I knew he was about to take me on. No matter how many times we had sex, I still had to adjust to his size. Holding on to my waist, he entered me nice and slow before he picked up his pace. The way he was stroking me wasn't too slow, but not too fast. I felt every vein and curve he had and it drove me crazy.

"Sssss. Remind me whose pussy this is?" he hissed, hitting my spot.

"It'sssss… mine."

"Face down!" he barked, pushing my face down into the bed. "Put your hands behind your back."

195

Doing as told, I put my hands behind my back only for me to feel cold steel again them. He stopped long enough to lock the handcuffs in place before he started to torture me again with long, deep strokes.

"Fuckkk," I moaned out.

"Shut up! And you better not nut either," he demanded, causing me to moan out louder.

"Didn't I say shut up? You got two options. Tap out and admit it's mine or take this dick."

Positioning my leg in the crook of his arm, he found my g-spot and went to work. I couldn't run in the position I was in if I wanted to. He had my leg and my hands hostage.

"Whose pussy is this?" he asked again.

"I'm about to nutttt."

"I wish you would. Ask."

"Babyyy… pleaseeee?"

"Please what?"

"Fuckkkkk."

"Say it and I'll let you," he groaned, releasing my leg and pushing me flat onto the mattress. I wasn't sure what it was about this position, but it drove me insane.

"It's yourrrssss! Blueeee, I'ma cummmm."

"Nut," was the only word he spoke and like a good little girl, my body obeyed. I felt his dick swell up inside me and it sent me over the edge. Dozing off as I felt my hands being released from the hands cuffs, I felt the bed move as Orion got out the bed but I couldn't keep my eyes open.

"I love you, Kylani," was the last thing I heard before I passed out.

Chapter 36: Blue

Kylani went to her dad's wake this morning. It was well into the afternoon and she was still gone. I still felt bad about last night, so me and Zane threw a BBQ for her to take her mind off of everything. When Piranha agreed to let us use his spot for it, we went all out.

Anything that could be placed on a grill, we had it. Steak, hamburgers, pork chops and chicken as well as corn, baked beans, baked macaroni and cheese and corn on the cob, we had it all. We knew that she only had us, so we invited the whole hood out to come kick it with us.

By the time La texted me saying that she was on the street, the party was in full swing. There were people everywhere and the music was bumping. Going out front to meet her, I made it out just as she was getting out the truck.

"What's up, baby girl? How you feeling?" I asked her, pulling her into a hug.

"I'm good, and why are all these cars out here?"

"Come on and I'll show you." I grabbed her handing leading her inside.

Just as I knew they would, everyone welcomed her and the fellas' ol' ladies were trying to include her. I sat back and watched, drinking a beer. The world seemed to be lifted off her shoulders as she sat around the pool laughing and joking and I'm happy I could help put that smile there.

"Ayo, Blue. Let me holla at you for a minute," Zane said, tapping me on the shoulder.

"Alright, here I come," I told him, stealing one last look at La before I followed him into the house.

Following behind him as he led the way to Piranha's office, both Bullet and Piranha were already waiting on us.

"What's up?" I asked once we sat down.

"Has La said anything about whether she was taking her place as the head of the family?" Zane asked.

"Nah, and I really haven't asked her again since before. When she ready then she'll let me know."

"You might want to ask her again."

"Why is that?" I questioned with my eyebrow raised.

"Her dad's death wasn't an accident. The doctor from the hospital called not too long ago and told me it was only a matter of time before Kye died. Apparently, he had been being poisoned for months and it finally caught up with him the night he died," he explained.

"Are they sure?"

"Yea. I think he knew he was dying though."

"Damn," was all I could say. I wouldn't put shit past her family at this point. I wasn't exactly sure how to tell her what I knew, but I knew that if she didn't take over that she was as good as dead. There were no ifs, ands or buts about it.

"Blue! Blue!" I heard someone yell my name from the hallway. Opening the door, I saw that it was Zak's ol' lady, Tammi.

"What's wrong?"

"It's La. She out there about to kill that girl. Come on."

Running back out to the yard, shit had gone left in the matter of minutes. Spotting the chick Brie that Kylani had found at my apartment that day, I knew shit was bad.

Kylani was on top of ol' girl giving her the straight business and I swear the punches she gave her was making my head hurt. The more I tried to get La off of her, the harder she hit.

"LA, LET GO!" I yelled, yanking her as hard as I could without hurting her.

"Get the fuck off of me, Orion! I thought you said that you didn't fuck this bitch?" she asked, looking at me with hurt in her eyes.

"I didn't fuck her. What the fuck are you talking 'bout?" I asked, looking at her confused.

"Tell her what you told me, baby. Tell her how she was young minded and insecure and that you need a real woman in your life," Brie said, staggering to stand up.

"Brie, you out of line," I warned, shooting daggers in her direction.

"How am I outta line? I was just telling her the truth before she attacked me. I didn't tell the bitch to be so sensitive."

My grip on La must have been too loose because she hit baby girl with a three-piece combo that made my head hurt. I didn't understand why bitches caught feelings when they knew shit was never that deep. Grabbing Kylani back into a bear hug, I whispered in her ear trying to calm her down.

"You wildin', La."

"Get the fuck off of me Blue before I hit your ass next," she warned.

"Not until you calm down and you ain't that stupid. I told you when you first met, hit me and I hit back."

"Whatever." She caught an attitude and sucked her teeth.

When I felt she was calm enough, I let her go. Just for her to storm off and go in the other direction out of the yard. She'd be alright, I'll handle that later, but for now I needed to handle the shit that was in front of me.

"Zane, go check on La for me. Tell her I'll be there in just a second," I told him, keeping my eyes on Brie.

"Sis gone' shoot both of y'all and I ain't trying to be an accomplice to murder," he chuckled, walking in the direction that La stormed off in.

"Y'all clear out. Let me holla at Brie for a minute."

It took everyone all of two minutes to clear out and when they did, I walked closer to Brie and wrapped my hand in her hair pulling her head back so she could understand that I meant every word I spoke.

"Let's be clear on something. You ain't nothing more than a two bit hoe that sucked my dick for two zans and some pills. Why the fuck do you think I would ever wife a bitch like you? If I wasn't as drunk as I was, I would never have touched your bum ass. I'm telling you this once and I hate to repeat myself. Stay the fuck away from me and my ol' lady because I'd hate to see your face on the front of the newspaper. Do I make myself clear?"

Something was seriously wrong with this bitch because instead of seeing fear in her eyes, I saw nothing but lust. This hoe had to be crazy, and that was one thing I didn't need in my life.

"Yes sir, daddy," she moaned, licking her lips.

"Keep playing with me and see what the fuck I do," I told her, pushing her away from me.

"Well, I hope you plan on being a father to your child."

"Don't try it. I didn't even fuck you."

"You didn't have to. You should really learn how to flush your own condoms," she laughed before walking off. "I really have to be going because I need to go check on *our* child."

If there wasn't a possibility that she was pregnant with someone's kid for real, then I would have hit her ass with a double tap to the dome. Running my hand over my face, I blew out a breath of frustration and tried to figure out what the fuck could possibly go wrong next.

Chapter 37: Kylani

Orion must have seen stupid stamped across my forehead. It took everything in me not to kill that bitch where she stood. I knew she looked familiar when she walked in the back yard, but I thought nothing of it until the bitch opened her mouth.

I was sitting with Tammi on the side of the pool laughing at some video on Facebook. DC Young Fly was clowning Raven hard as hell from the comments she made about not being an African-American. I didn't understand her because she wanted to be accepted by these white people and they would never give a fuck about her.

"Hi," I heard someone say from above me.

"Hey," I spoke, looking up at her.

"Don't I know you from somewhere?" she asked, sitting beside me.

"Nah, I don't think you do."

"I swear I've seen you before. Oh yeah ,I remember now. You came over to my boyfriend's apartment by accident one night."

"Boyfriend?"

"Yes. Blue. That was his apartment door that you knocked on. Well, I should say baby daddy now. I just found out that I'm five weeks pregnant," she said, rubbing her imaginary baby bump.

"Brie, don't come over here with that messy shit. You know that Blue would never fuck you," Tammi told her.

"I'm curious as to how your five weeks pregnant by him when I was with him five weeks ago?" I questioned.

"Oh, Blue wanders around with his little hoes from time to time, but he knows where home is," she smirked.

Something inside of me snapped, and I punched her as hard as I could, trying to wipe the smirk off her face. I must have blacked out because next thing I knew I heard Orion's voice and him trying to pry me off of her.

When I turned around to look at him, I tried masking the pain in my eyes while searching his for the truth.

"Get the fuck off of me, Orion! I thought you said that you didn't fuck this bitch?" I snapped, trying to wiggle out of his arms.

"I didn't fuck her! What the fuck are you talking 'bout?" he asked, looking at her confused.

"Tell her what you told me, baby. Tell her how she was young minded and insecure and that you need a real woman in your life," she said, trying to stand up.

I could hear him say something to her, but my mind wasn't processing it at all. All I could think about was rearranging her face and when he lifted his arm that was all it took for me to get back over to her and hit her ass again.

"Hey, sis. You alright?" Zane asked, pulling me from my thoughts.

"Yea. I'm straight."

"Let me find out you the next Lala Ali," he joked, getting in a boxing stance.

"Shut up Zane!" I laughed, throwing the Styrofoam cup that was in the cup holder at him.

"You know Blue didn't fuck that girl, right?"

"Then how is she pregnant?"

"Pregnant?" he asked confused.

"That's what she said."

"Nah. I don't believe that. You can't believe everything you hear. Females will say any and everything to get underneath your skin. Let that shit roll off your back."

Opening my mouth to respond, I closed it again when I saw that bitch walk out the backyard and blow a kiss at me. She better be glad that Zane was blocking the car door because if not, I would have whopped her ass again. Thirty seconds later, Blue came waltzing his ugly ass out too. He looked pissed off and he better be glad I couldn't find my gun when I came out here or I would have shot his ass in the kneecaps.

"Good looking out," he told Zane, dapping him up.

"Fix this shit, man. Call me when y'all make it home. See ya, sis."

Rolling my eyes at him as he got in my truck, it took all my self-restraint not to slap the fuck out of him.

"I didn't fuck that girl, La."

"Then how did she end up pregnant?" I asked, facing his direction.

"IF she even is pregnant. It ain't mine. She sucked my dick, nothing more nothing less," he said, looking me in the eyes. I wasn't sure why, but I felt like he was telling the truth.

"For your sake, she better not be," I warned. He didn't know it yet, but I would kill her and bury him in her blood. They could test my crazy if they wanted to, but I was sure they wouldn't like the outcome.

"Take me home. I've had a long day and I have an even longer day tomorrow."

Obliging to what I asked, he started the truck and headed home without another word. I couldn't catch a break and I felt like tomorrow would just be worse.

* * * *

Funeral Day…

Orion offered to come inside with me to the funeral, but this was something I had to do alone. They say everyone handles grief differently and I guess that was true. I asked that he just stay in the car and that I would text him if I needed him, but I knew that he wouldn't listen because when I got ready to get out he was right behind me.

The church was packed with what I'm guessing were people that knew my dad or knew of him. There were so many people that some of them had to stand against the wall. To keep up with appearances, I sat with my mom, Amari and Rylan on the front row, but when my mom reached over and patted me on the shoulder, I wanted to slap the hell out of her.

Most of the funeral was a blur as the pastor did his home going sermon. I was proud of my mom for not putting on her theatrics, but as soon as the pastor called everyone up for the final viewing, that went out the window.

I was almost embarrassed because she was falling all over him and trying to get in the casket and these people were eating it up. All I could do was shake my head. I don't doubt she was hurt, but she was doing the absolute most.

Since my dad was getting cremated, we didn't have to go to the graveyard and I was more than ready to leave. We sat on the front row as everyone came to offer their condolences.

"How you feeling?" Orion whispered, squeezing my thigh lightly.

"I'm just ready to go home," I told him, laying my head on his shoulder.

"It's almost over," he replied, kissing me on the top of my forehead.

Feeling someone's eyes on me, I looked up and met the eyes of a tall, dark skinned man with dreads and black shades covering his eyes. When he walked in our direction, I felt Orion tense up underneath me.

"La, we need to go. I'll be outside," he said, standing up and walking out the church.

I wasn't sure who this man was, but something about him seemed off. Like he had a black cloud hanging around him or something.

"I am so sorry fur you lose. I knew you father for a long tim." His accent was there, but I could still understand what he was saying.

"Thank you Mr...?"

"You can call me Carlos. If you ever need anyting, don't hesitate to ask," he smiled, handing me a business card and patting me on the shoulder.

Watching him as he walked out the side door of the church, I stood to my feet just as the last person exited the church.

"Are you not going to speak to your mother?" Leilani asked. "You should be nicer to me. I am the only parent you have left since your precious daddy is dead," she said chuckling.

"He wasn't just my daddy. He was your husband you sadistic bitch," I seethed, glaring at her. That mourning wife facade she was just doing a few minutes ago was completely gone.

"Oh, please. Kye was just a means to an end," she said, causing Amari and Rylan to laugh too.

"What's that supposed to mean?"

"Oh, you'll learn soon enough," she said laughing.

"Whatever, I don't have time for this." I turned to walk away.

"La?"

"What?" I asked, looking over my shoulder.

"If you walk out that door, you will be dead to this family and I can no longer protect you."

"Are you threatening me?"

"Not a threat, just telling you the truth," she smirked.

As I walked out, I could hear them laugh and the sound was getting under my skin. The way she laughed when she was talking about my father's death let me know that she knew more than she let on and if this bitch had anything to do with his death, I'd make her regret the day she came out of her mother's slimy ass pussy.

Descending the steps of the church, I saw Orion and the crew waiting on me and I knew what I needed to do.

"I'll do it," I told Orion when he came to meet me halfway.

"Do what?"

"I'm going to take over the Family," I responded.

I was tired of people playing with me and the ones that I loved. I'm about to show them what it means to be a Vendetti. Allow me to reintroduce myself. My name is Kylani Vendetti, and I'm about to be these motherfuckers' worst nightmare.

To be Continued...

CPSIA information can be obtained
at www.ICGtesting.com
Printed in the USA
LVOW12s0813041016
507217LV00002BA/255/P